←

TRANSFIXED

GOD | ROMANCE | TRAGEDY | FAMILY

PB Hawks

ISBN: 10:0692688587
ISBN 13:978-0692688588

For information contact;
http://www.pbhawksimpact.com

Book Cover was designed by Elsbro

First Edition: April 2016

←

←

DEDICATION

I dedicate this book to all believers who know, that they don't walk alone in this world. Even if evil surrounds us we have a power in us that is greater than anything the world can throw at us.

←

←

←

←

←

TRANSFIXED

←

←

ACKNOWLEDGMENT

This book is dedicated to my beautiful wife who I owe my life. Her love and her wisdom gave me the courage to complete books I didn't know I could write. With Gods Love for me and the Holy Spirit leading me along the way.

←

←

←

←

TRANSFIXED

CONTENTS

←

PROLOGUE

Peace and clam is what eyes bring to mind when you look at the town of Shadow. Located on the West coast of Oregon it gives off its beauty with the easygoing of a cool breeze coming from the ocean. Charming and quint is what most would say when their mind ponders the appeal and winsomeness of this town. It is said the beauty of this town is hard, if not impossible, to describe, but nevertheless even if the effort falls short the image begins to paint a picture that brings clam to our souls.

The residents of this town will go about their daily toil unaware of the evil that is about to befall them. The effects of this evil will echo trough very corner of their lives. The shock will effect everyone even though only four family's will be hurt. Evil of this magnitude can impact the residents for some time to come. How does anyone prepare for an evil impact as this town is about to face? There is no answer to such a question. You face evil by doing what is good in the eyes of the Lord. You face evil by treating others with love and sheltering them, as you would need to be cared for.

Take Jim Amico, when he came to town a few short months ago he brought a gentleness that nobody saw coming. Soon Jim started to show what he was made of by taking an interest in the young kids that surround the town of Shadow. He began to establish a baseball league that would touch the lives of kids from nine to thirteen. Not only did the town of Shadow benefit from his efforts but even towns that surround Shadow. It sent waves of hope and joy to those who live in Western Oregon.

Amy Jordan a young beautiful girl with a smile that could light up your heart and the energy of young lioness. Amy lived on a farm with her family. She was born in Shadow and has never went outside of the town except for the surrounding towns in 25 mile radius. Just next to her family farm was a farm just like the one she lives on. The lonely difference was the farm is owned by the Sky family. Part of the Sky family was a young man named Patrick. As children Amy and Patrick became friends, went to school, became boyfriend and girlfriend and eventually married. They had two children together, Summer and Jackson. Patrick joined the Army soon after graduation from High School. When the Iraq war began he was sent to join an elite corp of men who were required to perform secret missions across Iraq. In one of the secret missions Patrick was killed trying to save one his men. The news of his passing away drove a knife in the heart of the Sky family. After moaning the death of her husband and the father of her children what could she do? Amy quickly started to look for work and a job cleaning homes in the lake area of Shadow, than moved into a job with the local restaurant and raised her children working sometimes double shifts.

Summer is as beautiful as her mother, at the age of fifteen. The guys at school were always trying to get her to go out with them. Summer was shy and devoted to her church and her Lord, Jesus Christ. Her closeness to her mother and her brother kept her full and no need for the outside forces. Her mother taught her the goodness of God and his son Jesus Christ as they as a family studied the Bible. Her beauty is truly complete both inside and out.

Jackson was young and just wanted to play sports with his friends. He did not excel in his school work and is moody ever since his father passed away. Than Jim Amico came into town and started the little league Baseball. All of sudden he became outgoing and engaging with friends and school took on a higher importance in his life. He is a good ball player and an assist to his team. His only mountain to get over is his ability to freeze in place not moving anything, not even blinking, on occasions without any warning. He has been looked at by a multitude of doctors without any conclusions. They could not find anything wrong. So whats causing these episodes?

This newly formed family will go through many crazy attacks, but with the of help of God find their way through.

1

SUMMER IS MISSING

The ground is soggy and somewhat messy after a gigantic rainfall that seemed endless! Here in Oregon, the rainy season seems to occur throughout the year, but not always during the summer months. The woods are impassable, and the night is approaching fast. Jim knew to persist with the search during the night would be counterproductive. The search is for a young teenage girl named Summer Sky (Amy's daughter), unaccounted for...at that point, less than twelve hours since reporting her missing If she could not be found by early the next day, the outside chance of finding her alive will be slight, at best. But Jim couldn't just stop now, since there is no way he could tell the woman (Amy) who made his life so exciting and 'new,' that he will give up trying to find her daughter for the night! "NO WAY!" he thought. However, he must return home to get a better flashlight and warmer clothes.

Summer struggling against the ropes and tape that bind her. The deep-seated fear that she is experiencing seems overwhelming as the man holding her prisoner kept dragging her forward. Wondering what he would do next, keeps her anxious and agitated! She prayed: "GOD! PLEASE get me out of this situation NOW! I can't go on much longer!" She must also be wondering about the whereabouts and condition of the three other girls who had been with her...did the kidnapper kill them or hurt them in any way? She thought about the man (Jim) who might become her step-father and she must be hoping that he is doing everything he could to find her! Summer has been hoping for an answer to her prayer when, as she recounted later, she is pushed up some steps that seemed like the front of a porch. The kidnapper then took off the hood that prevented her from seeing anything around her. The house seemed dilapidated and gave her a feeling of 'cold!' He grabbed her and pushed her up the stairs leading to the second level where they entered an even colder, darker room. She is still bound as he began to take her clothes off. He is

strong and she fought against him. He then removed all her clothes ripping and cutting when
needed and pushed her onto the bed. She is lying
on her back and entire body is exposed. He then
began to tie her to the bed. The cold, damp room
frightened her even more! She experienced a
heightened awareness of the smell of 'putrefied
ruin' that reminded her of a dungeon in some old
dark castle! 'How am I going to get out of this';
she thought. She remembered reading in a police
novel that going along with her captor could lead
to an opportunity for a possible means of escape!
She is so embarrassed, she never experienced
her clothes off in front of a man and she asked
her Lord for help. She felt his presence holding
her in His arms. Her captor undressed and
jumped on the bed and soon on top of her, his
hands moving about her body, the terror is now
at fever pitch, she closed her eyes and braced
herself. The sexual act is over. It was over almost
as soon as it began, not for Summer, the whole
act is most horrifying, painful and something she
would not ever   forget.

Ever since she first heard of her missing
daughter, Amy couldn't think of anything except
her precious daughter's return home, safe and
sound! Thoughts of her possibly being abused
kept her in a state of constant terror. She was

thinking why did I agree to allow her to go on this camping trip with her friends in the nearby woods? Summer Sky is fifteen years of age and a beautiful girl. Her figure is slim and shapely. She would be attractive to any boy or man. Now because of Amy's negligence, she may lose her beautiful daughter forever! Her only hope is for Jim to find Summer before any harm could come to her!

Jim Amico arrived in town about six months ago with the hope of making this town his home. Jim and Amy met while her son Jackson is playing baseball in a league started by Jim and Bill (Bill is Jim's partner). After dating a few times, they fell in love.

Amy's was married to Patrick Sky, her high school sweetheart. He became an Army officer and laid down his life in Iraq during a 'Black Ops' mission. The news that Amy and the kids received five years ago almost destroyed them!

She never thought she could fall in love again, but her loneliness gave way to meeting this exciting architect from California. The last few months overwhelmed her and she couldn't remember how long it's been since she experienced this kind of happiness!

Jim went home from his trying search, made a pot of coffee, showered and put some warm clothes on and garbed his boots and a cup of coffee and started out the door. Reaching for his truck's door handled, a voice yelled out to him. "Hey Jim" the voice cried out. When Jim looked around he could see his partner Bill coming his way.

"Where are you going at this time of night?" said Bill. "I can't stop looking for Summer just because its night time!" Jim shouted back. "Then let me come with you!" Bill insisted. "OK, can you take some flashlights and batteries and are you dressed warm?" asked Jim. "Yes" said Bill. Jim became insistent: "Then why are you holding me up? Let's go!" Bill responded, "Where do think she might be?" Jim replied, "Perhaps we should start at the place where their camp site is," On the way, they came across an abandoned truck. It is a dark-blue Ford F-150...and very dirty! "Do you know this truck?" Jim asked. "Never seen it before," said Bill. Then he went over and knocked some mud off the truck's rear license plate. "Hey Jim! This truck's got California plates." Jim thought that the Highway Patrol should be notified so they could put a 'tracer' on it. "I'll make the call," said Bill. Much to their welcomed surprise, a Highway Patrol car came into view...and five minutes later, the Patrol car came rolling up. Officer Patrick Able and his partner Paul Evans is an old friends of Bill's. "Any idea who owns this truck?" Jim asked, "No! But we can place a call to California right now." A few minutes went by when Pat said, "It belongs to a drifter named Sid Naps. He's been going up and down this coast for at least a year or so since he lost his wife and daughter in a drunk-driving accident, and he happened to be the one driving the car." Jim asked, "How do you guys know this?" Pat said, "We picked him up a few times for 'disorderly conduct,' then let him go." Jim shouted, "You're kidding me! This could be the guy that is holding the girls!" Pat said, "Calm down!" Jim responded, "Look Pat, if this is your daughter, you wouldn't be so calm!" Pat reacted with: "We don't even know if this guy encounter the girls!" Jim replied, "Maybe not, but he's the only suspect we've got right now!" Bill intervened and said, "OK, let's set out on foot from this point and see if we come across anything!"

The campsite the girls chose is in a little clearing about 150 feet from the road. The tent they were preparing to erect was laid out and their sleeping bags were still rolled up on the ground. There were more of their belongings lying around "Jim said," There's nothing more we can do here." They started moving through the overgrown wooded area hoping to find something that would give them some clue about what happened to the girls. Along with Summer Sky, there were Genial Simms, Pam Joseph, and Ann Potter...all from the town of Shadow. They wanted to celebrate Pam's birthday and go camping. Four girls growing up fast! They wanted to be 'on-their-own' for a few days and get a taste of what it would be like being older. Seemed like a simple request from four good girls. As Jim and Bill continued their search, the Highway Patrol stayed with the abandoned truck, hoping the owner would show up. Hours went by with nothing new being reported. The sun was beginning to break the horizon, and the beauty of a brand new morning was obscured by the sadness they were feeling. They were moving on with their, 'last-bit-of-strength' when they came across a piece of torn clothing of some kind! It looked like a shirt...blue with white dots...a female garment without a doubt. They pressed on further into the woods. All of a sudden, they heard some faint, 'crying-like' sounds...then they literally 'almost stumbled' upon three girls tied to a large tree! These were some of the missing girls! Dirty, disheveled and bound together to a tree! They were crying and cold. They 'shouted-out' when Jim and Bill came into their sight! The joy of finding them was exhilarating, but was overshadowed by the realization that SUMMER WAS NOT WITH THEM!

The two men began to untie the girls while asking questions about Summer. Tears of joy were running down their faces. One girl said that the 'kidnapper' told them that he'd return shortly, but it had been a very long time since he took Summer with him! The girls indicated that Summer was his favorite. The man was wearing dirty jeans, a red shirt, cowboy boots...and he had on a mask. As their stories unfolded, it became obvious that the man 'kidnapped' the girls soon after they set up camp. He also had a gun, so they did whatever he wanted. Summer gave him a hard time, and he struck her on her head with his gun! She went down immediately and didn't move for about fifteen to twenty minutes! When she did awake, she was rubbing her head and told her friends how bad it hurt! "What did he do to you?" Jim asked. Genial said "His hands were all over us after he tied us up; he said he was 'checking for weapons.' I know that wasn't true because it didn't seem like he was checking for anything...he was just 'groping' and enjoying himself." Jim looked at Bill and said, "You take them back to the Highway Patrol so they can give a statement. Then take them home to their parents. Tell officers Pat and Paul that I'm continuing the search for Summer. Tell them we need to set up a search party right away! If nothing comes up, I'll be home after it gets dark. I'll contact their station-house to discuss the details!" Bill nodded and led the girls back to the truck.

Jim was shattered inside! The worst night-mare anyone could've imagined had actually be-come a reality! They had at least found three of the girls...now 'safe' but definitely 'shaken-up!' They must now find Summer...still missing and undoubtedly traumatized. Jim did the only thing he could: he pressed on looking for the child who most likely was, at that very moment, being abused by a very evil man. Before he continued on, he stopped, knelt down and asked the Lord to direct him along the way and guide him to where they are. He kept up his pursuit and found some other pieces of clothing that were 'bloodied' and torn. He became more fearful...and it was getting colder! The darkness of the night was closing in, and he felt as if it was time to go home, get some rest, maybe take a shower, change clothes and start 'new' the next day. "IMPOSSIBLE!" he thought. "Not going to happen! Got to get back out there! Can't 'rest' now...need to get some help to find her! I'll call Pat or Paul at the station! Got to set up the Search Party!"

He got to the road and hitched a ride into

town. When he arrived home, the town treated him like a hero and welcomed him home. He reminded them "it was not over yet! There's still a lot of searching to do! There's another girl named Summer Sky still out there and it won't be over until she's home safe also! Yes! We can be happy that three beautiful girls were found in pretty good shape...and when you thank the Lord for these blessings, don't forget 'Summer' still needs to be in your prayers!"

2

DREAMING JIM REMINISCES

The temporary comfort of being home was overshadowed by the despair of missing Summer. The doorbell rang, and Amy was standing in front of him as he opened the door. With tears streaming down her face, she cried out: "JIM! What do we do now?" and pressed into his arms. He could feel the terror she was feeling, trembling and shaking he took her in his arms and did his best to comfort her is some way. "We keep searching, sweetheart, we just don't give up! We keep looking and caring until the day she walks back into our home," Jim reassured her. Distraught, she said, "Jim, I don't know what to do!" Totally exhausted, they both sat down on the sofa. We pray to our God, He is the one in control. Jim held her tight and said, "Yes you do...we persist in praying and trusting that the Lord will protect her and show her the way back into our arms." He told Amy that even though he needed to get some sleep, he was going to get some help and get back out on the search. Although Amy was not part of the search the waiting took a toll on her strength, their exhaustion took over and they both fell asleep right there on the sofa!

'Dreams' are sometimes a comfort...sometimes terror-ridden! Reliving one's past is traumatic as it gets, going over the things you could have done and didn't, or the things you did do and are sorry for but can't change. We won't know Jim's and Amy's dreams (comfort or terror) until they awaken from a short sleep brought on by this incredibly traumatic event! Jim has always had a robust dreams and it seems that the more difficult or demanding life becomes the more detailed his dreams become. Nothing in Jim's life has been more dramatic than what is happening right now. In Amy's case her daughter is as important as you can imagine. Our lives are full of dreams, but in some it illuminates the future.

Jim's life, to many, may seem rather 'ordinary.' It began simply enough, in a small part of a large city. He was born 'James Amico' to an Italian Catholic family in South Brooklyn, a borough of New York City. Brooklyn is the most populous of New York City's five boroughs. As far as he could remember, they always lived close to his grandmother and grandfather on his mother's side of the family. His father was a construction laborer and worked as hard as you can imagine, however, didn't bring home a heap of money. In most Italian families, the mother or the wife takes care of the money: pays the rent, pays all the bills and buys the groceries. Jim's family was no different. The Amico family moved a lot when he was young and Jim didn't understand the reason at that time. Perhaps it was because his mom always tried to keep the household expenses low and continued to look for places where the rent was a little lower. Jim's mom was always worried about money. As a construction laborer, his dad worked only when it didn't rain or snow. That meant that work in the winter months was very 'sparse,' which made it very stressful when it came time for his mom to pay the bills. Nevertheless, it was difficult for Jim also, constantly finding new friends and adjusting to different schools. His earliest memories were of their lives as they lived in what his family called "the projects," which consisted of a cluster of five-story buildings spread over a multi-block area. That's where he spent his younger years. His family then moved a few streets from his grandfather's house and stayed in that area until Jim dropped out of High School and enlisted in the United States Army.

This neighborhood was made up of what were called "Brownstone Houses,' with outside stairs that led to the second floor. Row-after-row of these types of homes lined most of the streets in the area. The homes were 'luxuriant' in terms of today's standards. The craftsmanship, quality and details are not seen in homes built today. Unfortunately, most people inhabiting those dwellings didn't appreciate the 'quality' that was all around them. The interior consisted of the most exquisite carpentry this era had seen: solid wood moldings at the floors and ceilings...all carved wood with door and window frames that would take many hours to complete in today's work-environment.

Even the special trim was made from the best wood one could buy. Jim and his family were living in the style of 'millionaires' and didn't even know it!

Jim liked this neighborhood; he had friends just a block away. It was far enough away that his family couldn't interrupt him during the day...and close enough that when he had to be home at a certain time, he could make it in just a few minutes. This is where Jim spent most of his teen years outside of his home. The hot summer days were spent on the street playing ball or sitting on the steps of a shady Brownstone with his friends (boys mostly, girls when it was OK to be seen with the boys). Jim attended Catholic School from the first to the eighth grades. "Brothers" taught him and they didn't put up with much 'fooling around' as they described it. So you can count on being attacked, ah...I mean, 'hit' with a ruler or a belt at some point in the day. They taught him about God as emanated from their way of thinking (or should I say, the 'Catholic Way'). Jim remembers they didn't have much of an 'accommodating spirit' with kids like Jim that were a little slower than the core-group. Yet, they asked why 'those kids' weren't doing well in their classes...as if they really cared. Jim struggled through school and always felt he was behind all of his classmates. So, going to High School was very scary and nerve-racking. It would be very difficult for Jim to explain to someone when he was asked "Why" he was behind. How do you tell someone that you 'just didn't get it' when they had successfully taught the others...or 'I needed a little more time' to get it? You feel like you're 'made differently' from the others. Jim found himself skipping school a lot, "playing hooky," as it was called back then...until a letter from school to his parents soon disclosed the situation. His parents knew that learning was an important part of life and without it, what kind of work would he be able to do? His mom would say, "Do you want to be like your father and break your back the rest of your life?" Nobody wanted that, so his parents gave him the option to either "get a firm grip on yourself and finish High School," or go into military service (in this case, the Army)...take his GED and get a High School Diploma that way. A High School Diploma was the least amount of schooling for a worthwhile job back then.

Giving it as much thought, as he knew how, at the age of seventeen Jim decided to join the Army instead of finishing High School at home. If he stayed at home and tried to finish High School, it would be more of the "same-old'-grind." No one was crazy about his choice, but they went along with it. Jim dropped out of High School, enlisted in the Army on his birthday and started his military career. Jim was all of seventeen and his understanding about 'life' was somewhat 'incomprehensible' in his own mind. He truly had no idea of what life would be like in the Army; he just knew that it would be different...and that it was.

He went through and passed the necessary medical exams, and was sworn into the Army and assigned to Fort Dix, New Jersey. He completed his 'basic training,' which was a feat in itself, and received orders to report to Fort Sill, Oklahoma. After a two-week stay at home, he flew to the 'great out-doors' of Fort Sill. He found that this would be decent training, since he enjoyed operating and maintaining the 'heavy howitzers.' This experience made him think about being 'in war' and how that might feel. After completion of his artillery training he received orders from Baumholder, Germany. He had a month's leave and he enjoyed every minute of it...after all, it would be a long time before he would see home again. Jim relished the fact that the United States was, at that time, between the Korean and the Vietnam wars. Although he didn't realize it then, this put him in quite a favorable position!

With all of his family's moves, he had numerous opportunities to meet and get to know diverse kinds of people. They were from different nations and he was amazed by the colors of their skin. In that way, he wasn't 'inexperienced' compared to men who lived in areas that didn't have the diverse races to which he was exposed. Jim spent the next eight days on a ship that transported him to Germany. He met men from all over the US, sharing his experiences with them and learning from them and their experiences. Mostly though, he was eager to get off that ship! In retrospect, he found it to be a 'horrible' experience and he never wanted 'transportation' like that ever again! First, they had to clean every part of the area where they slept; then every day they had to go up on deck for hours at a time. The cold and 'biting' winds that blew on deck were re-lentless and very uncomfortable!

Germany was very different but very exciting! After leaving the ship, Jim was transported on a train that took him to Baumholder. That journey included beautiful mountain, views that he hadn't seen before...even in his travels in the US Coming from the inner city, this was a visual treat! Jim was assigned to the 24th Company Second Sec-tion, which would be his home for the next two-and-a-half years. When Denny Bolden, who was the Section Leader, set eyes on Jim and found out he was from Brooklyn, he called him into his of-fice. He looked at Jim and said, "So you're the punk from Brooklyn! First thing, go, get your hair cut...NOW!" Jim went IMMEDIATELY to the bar-ber on the base and got a short haircut (at least what he considered 'short')...and then went back to Sgt. Bolden, who took one look at him and said, "Get it shorter!" So off he went to make it 'military short.' He returned to Sgt. Bolden who was then 'basically satisfied.'

Sergeant Bolden was born in southern Missis-sippi to a single mother who had four other boys. His family was poor but they stuck together and made life happen...whatever it took! He was a tall, black man with stern features on his face which gave him an 'invulnerable sense of authority.'

Jim was given a bunk, a footlocker and a standing-locker. Then the guys showed him how to arrange his clothes and boots and shoes for inspection. While doing all this setting-up, it became time for lunch. Jim would never say an unkind word about anyone when describing them, such as any kind of racial remark regarding the fact that the guys and Sgt. Bolden are African-American men (not that it was somehow 'bad' to be African-American). Jim had been raised in neighborhoods where African-Americans were part of everyone's life; he never considered them to be any different from the way he is. So, when lunchtime arrived, he went to lunch with his new-found friends. Well, these times were in the early 1960s when whites and blacks were not exactly accustomed to sitting with each other. But Jim didn't give it a second thought since these men are his friends and one sits with one's friends; it doesn't make any difference if they are Black, Hispanics, and Asians...or whatever. As Jim observed his surroundings, he became aware of the fact that the white men were looking at him as if he had done something 'culturally unacceptable.' Regardless, he just continued to eat with his friends and that's the way it was, day after day. This news got around to everyone in the company and on the base that the new white boy was eating with blacks, but Jim didn't give it a 'second-thought' and led his life the way he always did. He simply went on treating everyone with respect, no matter what the color of his or her skin happened to be.

It wasn't long before Sergeant Bolden and Jim became close friends. He didn't know why his Sergeant took a liking to him... perhaps because he saw the 'need' in Jim. His Sergeant soon began to give him more responsibility along with more leadership in the section. He soon became an 'E5 Sergeant' and shortly thereafter, he was promoted to 'Second-in-Command' of the entire Second Section. This is where Jim learned his leadership skills.

Sgt. Bolden became the 'father-figure' Jim never had from his real father. His real father wasn't a bad guy at all; he made great efforts to supply his family with all they needed. His father had a difficult life. It's now known that he had a 'learning disorder.' As much as Jim's dad tried to learn how to read, and the truth is, he tried really hard to read, he just couldn't do it. His dad grew up being called 'stupid,' lazy and made fun of almost every day of his life. So his dad developed an 'attitude.' This attitude was intensely distrustful of everyone and he seemed like he was a terribly bitter man. In fact, he was a very affectionate and caring person. His brothers, sisters and extended family agreed and would tell this 'completely different story,' than other could see and that would include his own 'good friends.' Jim loved his father and just wanted to spend more time with him, but that just never seemed to work out. Later in Jim's life, he learned that his father had cancer...so he made time to be with him toward the end of his father's life. They took walks together and talked a great deal about things of the past. On one of these walks, Jim asked his dad why he never took him fishing or to a ball game (they were both big Brooklyn Dodger fans). His dad said something that broke Jim's heart: he said, "I never considered you liked me."

Even today, when he thinks about those words, it crushes him. He tried to tell his dad how much he loved him and how proud he was of his dad. He was so heartbroken that his dad felt that way; he took time to analyze his own behaviors. His dad was changing from that cynical attitude to one of compassion for everyone around him. God seemed to be preparing him for heaven. Jim's father died soon after his last visit with his son. This phase of his mothers' life was very hard on Jim's mother, so he stayed a few extra days, after the death of his father, with her until he knew she would be 'all right' living alone. His mom developed great friendships and support of the friends and neighbors she'd developed over many years.

Jim's time in the Army was ending. He began to prepare himself to head home and to enter the work force. This was 'frightening' in itself and 'living-at-home' until he could make it on his own was even more frightening. The exit from the military was effortless and occurred with no complications. His 'Honorable Discharge' seemed insignificant at the time. He didn't realize how important it would become as he started to look for work on the outside. So now this phase of his life was over...but a whole new adventure was just beginning.

3

JIM MOVES TO SHADOW

When Jim left the Army, he had a variety of different jobs until he made up his mind to go to school to study Architecture. So he took his military benefits and went to the best architectural school New York had. Seven years later he graduated with the top school awards (the extended length of seven years is because he worked during the day and went to school at night). He enjoyed and had a 'passion' for the architectural profession. 'Life' was exciting! Before he made the decision to leave the city, the company that employed him asked him to be part of a large hospital project. He agreed and was soon leading a group of talented men preparing architectural drawings for one of the biggest projects his firm ever designed. When the project entered the building phase, he was required to be 'on site' to instruct the contractor and to answer questions about the contract documents. This work was not only challenging but very difficult. Working with contractors is as tough as it gets because they are consistently discovering/identifying a 'need' to make 'modifications' resulting in 'change orders' which, in the process, sometimes makes the architect 'look bad.' So Jim had paper-work coming out of his ears, so to speak, and he was always in and around the building making sure the contractor was following the contact documents, as he should.

After twenty-five years, it was time for Jim to say 'good-bye' to New York City. He packed his car with bags of clothes and items he wanted to take. Saying good-bye to family and good friends is difficult because one never knows when one will ever see them again. His mom threw a big party with aunts, uncles and cousins including friends that he grew up with, as well as some of his 'associates' with whom he worked. Leaving the 'BIG CITY' had always been a dream of his ever since he returned from Germany. The city had great work, an up and coming Architect, and beautiful offices...but you had to put up with the traffic and 'crowds' on the streets and subways...virtually most everywhere you went! Jim wanted something like a small town with room to move-around...without feeling claustro-phobic...with 'landscaping' like trees, hills, lakes and rivers (also you must mention the 'fresh air!') Other tall buildings surrounding you on every side!

As I said before, that was twenty-five years ago! California was getting too crowded and he wanted to be somewhere else but didn't know where that might be. Then one day, a woman he was seeing invited him to go with her to her home state of Oregon. They decided to drive so they took his car because it was a 'convertible' and much more fun to drive! His girlfriend had lived in the western part of Oregon in a city called 'Shadow' before moving to California. The ride was long and not exciting at all since they were traveling on the I-5 Freeway. California is a big state and getting through it was not a very pleas-ant experience...that is, until they reached the city of Mount Shasta. They stayed in a small hotel with a view of that majestic mountain. The next day, they continued their journey and were dis-covering that 'views' were getting more interest-ing with each mile! The mountain ranges they traveled through were some of the most charm-ing and delightful sights Jim had ever seen! The hills and valleys were spectacular! First, a great 'ascent' was experienced...followed by just as great a 'descent.' They both loved the 'excitement' of each winding turn and the vistas of blue skies and greenery were beyond breath-taking! Four hours later, they reached their destination.

To get to the City of Shadow, they had to cross a magnificent bridge which gave them a view of the 'Old Town harbor' that was truly outstanding! Jim would see this same view many more times. She (Kim) arranged to stay at a 'Bed and Breakfast' in town by what was called the 'Winless River.' This 'B & B' was a beautiful place to stay... and the rooms were just as beautiful! Yes! I did say 'rooms!

Jim had previously never let himself get 'too serious' about any one woman because his profession 'ate up' most of his time. He wasn't like other men...sleeping around with whomever they could get into bed. He was raised with the belief that sex was for the marriage bedroom. He tried to live by that rule as much as he could. Besides, he was a very shy person most of his life. Jim is a good-looking man approaching 52 years of age with grey in the temple-area of his hairline. Most women would consider him attractive and handsome.

Kim showed Jim around the town...especially around the river area. She dropped by the home where she lived when her parents were alive. Kim lost her parents one cold and dreary night about three years ago when a drunk driver took their lives. Kim was understandably heartbroken over the loss of such an important part of her life. She went into a deep depression, which took more than a year for her to recover and start 'living' again. Jim was a big part of her recovery; his friendship was a stabilizing effect and allowed her to 'move-on' in life.

The sights of this beautiful city dazzled Jim and he told Kim that he thought that this could be the place he may choose to live! "What about your work?" was her return comment? Jim said, "I'll retire from architecture." Kim countered, "...and what will you do then?" What a question, Jim thought. He'd been an architect for so many years, but recently, perhaps even for the past several years, he'd become dissatisfied and lost some of his motivation because he was no longer a part of the 'design process' or the 'construction document preparation.' He had become a 'manager,' a position that was no longer involved in the 'creative' role of architecture...but simply the man who makes sure the project makes a profit. How could one spend seven years in school (plus all the classes needed to stay on course) and now only be responsible for the 'money part' of architecture? That's certainly not why he went to school! He wanted to be an architect...not an accountant. So, retiring and perhaps opening a small store or a small architect's office...or going into construction...was becoming much more attractive. He knew he had to complete his vacation, which had a few more days left, and return to his office and make his retirement decision 'official.' The days came and all-too-soon evaporated...and he became more convinced that 'retiring' was the right thing to do.

So the drive home was exhilarating, almost intoxicating and truly satisfying! Kim said, "You look happier than ever before!" He was gratified that he'd finally made up his mind to live somewhere he loved and do something that gave him pleasure...feelings similar to those he had right after graduation. No longer would he be anxious about the progress of the project or the profit-line or the salary-level of the people working on the project. Oh! He was wise enough to know that these things would always be part of his life in some form or another, but not a 'nervous' or 'edgy' part (at least those were the feelings that he hoped would result from his decision to retire. The 'farewell' at his office was 'one-to-remember' and all his associates gave him warm words of encouragement and even some tears of love!

The town of Shadow is small...much smaller than Jim was used to. That was OK with him, Jim thought. The town has a heart big enough to wel-come anyone and everyone who visits. The river, called 'Winless,' runs through it and is a 'sight-to-behold' and a beauty that salutes its residents each day.

Jim has lived in Oregon for a very short time now but has already fallen in love with a State that just pours-out its beauty in ways that keep its residents 'in awe!' This is said in truth...not to lure you to move to Oregon (heaven knows this state doesn't need more people)! The beauty in Oregon is hard to describe, but a brief example may suffice: when the sun comes out and shines itself on this land, the people have a chance to observe their surroundings. As described herein...the hills, valleys, trees, flowers, lakes, rivers, etc., all of God's created elements...are simply breath taking! These things being said, it all comes with a price. You need to be aware that during most of the fall and winter, the residents are burdened with rain that sometimes never ends (at least it seems that way at times).

To say Jim lives in 'paradise' is an understate-ment! Yet, there are too many people who just take it all for granted...abusing it whenever it suits them. When Jim observes the charm...the elegance...the grandeur of this town, it takes a positively exhilarating toll on his emotions! Yes, there are members of his family and good friends that he left behind, but to be frank, most likely he will never see them again. The distress of leaving them is surpassed by the magnificence and majesty of this 'little-piece-of-heaven' that he now calls 'home.' Jim sat enjoying his morning coffee when he was hit with another great idea!

The town of Shadow had many small places to buy coffee. It even had a Starbucks located in the Safeway market. Jim thought if he could build a coffee shop on the river where people could come in for a good cup of coffee and enjoy all the sights the river had to offer...well, that could be a 'welcome addition' to this 'little-piece-of-paradise!' His plan was to build a large deck out over the river's edge and at the back of his new 'coffee-house.' He would install huge windows so all could see the grandeur of God's creation! A large fireplace would be one of the attractions inside and would come in handy when it was too cold to go outside to enjoy the river. He was excited! He thought he would call the place "Hawks of the Day", because 'hawks' were bountiful around the river. Later, he thought better and just decided to call it "Hawks."

Jim knew that obtaining land from the local real estate agents would not be easy. He embarked upon this task as quickly as he could. Soon, agents were calling him day and night. He didn't mind because he needed as many agents looking as he could get. After many months of looking at property, Jim couldn't seem to find anything that would excite his imagination! All the properties he was shown were missing one or more of the 'essential elements' he believed were needed to make a totally successful project

One day while Jim was looking for a 'youth baseball organization' in which he could participate, he found out that the city did not have an organization that gave the youth a special place to play the 'great-game-of-baseball!' Jim loved baseball and considered starting up a league for kids from 9 to 13 years of age. He went to City Hall and asked the mayor if it were possible to start a league for the kids of this city. The mayor overwhelmingly supported the idea! Jim decided that he could 'carry the heavy load' since he realized that he had the city's support!

He and the city officials located an empty field and Jim started clearing away the brush, when some big guy (who was maybe 6 ft. 4 in. tall)

came over and asked him, "What are you doing?" Jim said, "Oh hi! I'm Jim 'Hawks' Amico." The tall guy said "Hi! My name's Bill." So Jim told him that he wanted to start a baseball league for the youth of their city...and this 'field' was as good a place as any to start! Bill responded, "You're new here, aren't you?" Jim answered, "Yes I am." Bill followed up with, "I heard around town that you were looking for some place to build a coffeehouse...is that right?" Jim said, "Yes...something like that...and I'd like to put it in 'Old Town' by the river if I could." Bill said, "I think I might be of some help." Jim asked, "How's that?" Then Bill said, "I have a lot in Old Town that I can't do anything with." So Jim asked, "Why's that?" Bill replied, "It's too small to get any use out of it." Jim then inquired, "How big is it?" Bill responded, "Well, when we get finished here, I'll show it to you." Jim was intrigued and enthused by Bill's words...and said, "Great!" They both started working together to clear the lot and before they knew it, they had cleared the entire lot! Bill pulled up his truck and they loaded the brush on the truck and took all of it to the dump. What relief Jim felt! It would've taken him 'alone' maybe four or five days to accomplish what he and Bill did in one single day!

Bill took Jim to see the lot he had on the river in Old Town. When Jim saw the lot, he had to 'try hard' to subdue his excitement! Bill told him that his property extended 50 more feet past the water line. Jim indicated that that was not a problem because he wanted to build a deck out over the river. Bill said, "That's why I can't use the lot, but putting a deck out there is a great idea!" Jim jumped ahead of himself and said, "How much do you want for your lot, Bill?" Bill responded, "I'd like to be part of the business, if that'd be OK with you." Jim scratched his head and said, "I never considered having a partner, but I'm receptive to the idea. Let's set a time and place to meet so we can develop an agreement." They decided to meet at Bill's house the following night. Jim was beside himself with excitement! In one day, he'd resolved two 'challenges' that he'd been working on for months! Thank you God!

He was on his way to Bill's house when he felt an 'urging' by the Holy Spirit, so he pulled over to the side of the road and prayed out loud: "Thank you, Lord...for the opportunity to have this meeting! Please guide me and help me as I talk with my new friend Bill." He then continued on toward his destination. When he arrived in front of Bill's home, he was shocked! "Just short of 'magnificent!' was his initial thought! It was a two-story house with a wrap-around porch; it even had a circular driveway with a three-car-garage! No exaggeration; it was bigger and more beautiful than he could have imagined!

Jim knocked on the door and Bill called-out: "Please come in!" The meeting began with Bill saying, "I'd like to start with a prayer, if that's OK." It went something like this: "Dear Father, we come before You in the name of Jesus, Your beloved Son. Please guide us through this challenging meeting and may Your will be done...in Jesus' name we pray, Amen."

Bill started the meeting by asking a very personal question...a question that most people would never initiate with someone so 'early' in their new relationship: "Do you believe in the Lord Jesus Christ?" Jim sat back in his chair and was speechless. "Wow!" Jim thought...'I didn't see that coming!" Jim responded by saying "Being a Catholic all my life, I would have answered, 'yes.' I was told about Jesus and God the Father, so yes...I believe in Jesus Christ." Bill said, "Let me put this in a different way. Have you asked Jesus to come into your heart and have you asked Him to cleanse you of your sins?" Jim responded, "No, I never knew I had to do that." Then Bill said, "Why did Jesus die on a cross?" Jim answered, "To save the world from their sin." Then

Bill said, "Let me ask you something, Jim. Did Jesus die for you?" Jim stopped to think about what Bill had said. He knew Jesus died for everyone and since he was part of everyone...then, "Yes. Jesus died for me. Why did you ask that question?" Jim wondered. Bill took another step and said, "Jim, if we are going to be in business together, then that is the most important question I could ask. You see, Jesus...and what He stands for...is more important than life itself!" Jim didn't know what to say. Was he dealing with a 'religious fanatic' or a sincere, Godly man? He didn't know how to go on from there, so he decided to be patient and see where their conversation was leading.

Bill didn't hold back...he continued on about his love for Jesus Christ: "I hope you don't take this the wrong way, Jim. I know that we haven't known each other very long...it's just been a few days. But I have a need to tell everyone I know about the love of Jesus. He showed us how to love and He showed us that our fellow man is more important than our own lives. In the beginning, He gave us the gift of 'Free Will' to choose 'good' over 'evil;' 'Life' over 'death.' So He came down from Heaven to this Earth that He created just for us...to give us 'Life' and His hope is that we choose 'Life!' Jim, this God we know and serve is 'perfect' and expects us to be 'perfect,' but He knew we could never be that perfect. So He asked His beloved Son to become human and die for the sin of the world...and Jesus said, 'Father, Your will be done.' Jim, Jesus was talking to a priest, a ruler of the Jews, named Nicodemus, in Israel...and told Him that he must be 'born again.' Let me read this excerpt in [John 3:1-7]." After Bill read the scriptural verses, he boldly asked Jim, "Do you want to receive Jesus right now...tonight...do you want to be 'born again?'"

Jim paused to think about what he had heard. He thought about the 'hunger' he had been feeling for God in recent days, how he longed to be close to the God who made him. Jim took all this into his mind and said, "Yes, I would like to be right with God." Bill responded, "That's great, Jim! Let's pray a prayer and you follow along with me, OK?" Jim nodded his head in approval. "Father, you sent your Beloved Son to save us from our sins. We ask Jesus to cleanse us from all unrighteousness and live in our hearts from now on. Make our souls as white as snow with your precious blood, Amen!"

Jim stopped and paused for a moment because he felt something... something new and different! He felt a new sense of 'love' in a way he couldn't explain! It felt as if someone was pouring it all over him! He fell to his knees with tears coming down his face! "What just happened?" he asked. Bill said, "You have now officially become a part of God's family! Jim, Sunday morning service begins at 10:30am and I hope we'll see you there!" Jim paused and said, "So what about our business agreement?" Bill said, "What do you have in mind?" Jim said, "I was thinking that we've each brought something good to the table...so what about a 50/50 deal?" Bill considered it and said, "That's too much for me, Jim. You'll be doing most of the work, you being an architect. I'm only putting in some money, so let's say a 60/40 split...60 is your portion and mine is 40. What do you say about that?" Bill replied. Jim responded with, "What? I didn't come here to take from you...I came to share an equal load!" Bill (in his magnanimous spirit) responded, "Jim, you are not 'taking' from me. Since we have known each other, you've given me more hope and excitement than I ever had! You put a 'spark' in me, son...that I haven't seen in years! If you don't believe me, ask my wife!" His wife, May, had just come in from another room and she enthusiastically joined the conversation with, "That's right, Jim...and I love it!" Jim just made the best deal he had ever made with the man who led him to a relationship with Jesus Christ! "What was going on?" he asked himself. "Wow! Lord, what will You do next?" Jim did go to the church service that Sunday and was introduced to many other Christians that live in Shadow.

4

THE LEAGUE BEGINS

Summer was coming fast and Jim had the new Baseball League all set up with tryout scheduled for that next Saturday. The field was in good shape thanks to the High School coach who gave Jim grass-seed and loaned him the watering equipment and the machine to make the foul lines. The grass, which no one ever thought would be ready, was looking so fine that people didn't even want to walk on it! Jim had worked diligently to prepare and pass out a pamphlet introducing all of Shadow's residents to the new youth baseball league.

The tryout was just a way to know 'who' and 'how many' of the kids and their families would show up. Jim hadn't realized that the pamphlet would reach numerous surrounding towns as well. He expected 50 to 75 kids to show up. Well, two hundred kids and their parents showed up! Jim was shocked and exhilarated! Thinking fast, he couldn't possibly tryout all these kids in one day, so he brought the crowd together and said, "Thank you all for coming! I must tell you I didn't expect this many young men and their families to be here! So I won't waste anyone's time! This is what we'll do: we'll take everyone's name, address, and phone number...I'll contact each of you during the first part of next week and set up a time with smaller groups so we can truly see the talent we have. Parents! Please take note: in order for this league to function properly, we need your participation! Without it, this new baseball league can't possibly be a success! So now, look around at this field your kids will be playing on! A snack bar will be built right there behind home plate. Don't be concerned about your kid's playing skills 'cause in this league, everyone will play in every game! I will need a committee to establish rules. We'll need managers, coaches, umpires and grounds-keepers. Experience doesn't matter. We'll teach you and your kids...and train anyone who needs training. Again, I thank you for coming! And now, please

start lining-up at home-plate and we'll begin taking your information."

Jim and Bill stood at home plate for some
time, each taking the names of the kids and their
parents. Jim did call each kid that showed up and
set up the morning and afternoon sessions with
about ten kids per session. That meant he and
Bill would set-aside several days for 'categorizing'
players. Bill took the afternoon sessions and Jim
took the morning sessions. It also gave them the
opportunity to watch the fathers as well as the
mothers for 'manager ship' and 'coaching' abili-
ties. To Jim's surprise, there were quite a few
who seemingly understood the game of baseball
(both parents and kids). He talked to these parents about a 'workable draft.' There were 210
kids, which would mean that there could be 15
kids per team and 14 teams. So he needed 14
managers and at least that many coaches. Definitely not an easy task! He set up the draft for a
Friday night and they'd meet in the boardroom at
the City Hall. The room was packed with parents,
impatient to participate! When all the smoke settled, each of the 14 teams had a 'full-roster' with
a manager and two coaches for each team. Jim
instructed the managers to have the names for
their teams by the following Wednesday so a
schedule could be put together for the upcoming

season. He talked to all the interested parents about their participation. He said the league would need help at the snack bar, field maintenance, umpires, etc. Jim also planned to have an announcer for each game (he first thought he would take care of the announcing, but then determined that that would be 'too much' for him to do at the start of a new league). The schedule would have one game each night of the week and two games on Saturday. Here in the Northwest, it stays 'light' longer in the summer than most other states, so Jim didn't think lights would be necessary at that time. He still had to get the snack bar built along with 'stands' for people to watch the game. He was able to secure three umpires for each game and two parents for snack-bar duty for each game. Jim and Bill would take good care of the grounds-keeping work until someone would volunteer. Jim and Bill then realized and were satisfied that all the things needed to start the season were sufficiently established! It was March 15 and the season would start on June 2nd, and end on August 23rd. That's 14 weeks of baseball for the kids: one game per week for each team and 98 games in total (14 teams = 7 games per week = 98 games total).

Jim's 'passion' for the game of baseball was oh-so-evident! He worked diligently to make this new league 'happen successfully' for the youth of this and surrounding towns...and he loved every moment! The vision had definitely been unfolding and he felt pride in what was being accomplished (thanks also to the invaluable help of so many other people, especially Bill)! Team practices were taking place all over the town of Shadow and in other nearby towns as well. Wherever there was an accessible space to play, the managers were practicing with their respective teams. Jim also decided to make a schedule for practices on the new ball-field that he and Bill put together. Each team had a chance to perform in the field on which they would play their games. He didn't realize that Bill already had the frame of the snack bar started and it'd be finished in a very short time. All of these concerted efforts were really happening! The excitement of the new League was spreading to all the people in the town of Shadow and nearby towns as well!

Jim had something else that was weighing heavily on his mind: the architectural plans for the development of the new coffeehouse! He took time to measure the lot Bill showed him and began to make some conceptual design drawings (including how the state-of-the-art deck would look). He sent the concepts to a structural engineer he was told about in the area. He requested a survey of the property to determine the exact boundaries and 'topographical grades.' His architectural mind was 'churning' and he felt a surge of joy that he hadn't sensed in a very long time! He completed his preliminary concepts and sat down with Bill and presented his plans to him. Bill was overwhelmed! He had never really gotten involved in the entire 'building-process' before (even when he worked with the contractor who built his own house). Bill soon began to figure out the 3-Dimensional results of what he was seeing through the concept plans. Bill exclaimed, "I never pictured it to be so streamlined and beautiful!" Jim said "We'll only use products from the local area: the wood, the rocks, metal, and such. The deck will be the 'focal-point' and the huge fireplace will be seen from both the street as well as the riverside of the building. What do you think, Bill?" Jim asked. "It's just plain 'great!' I love it!" exuded Bill. "OK then, I'll start the construction documents immediately!" Jim replied.

5

THE LAUNCH

After meeting with the Mayor and Mack Null, the director of the Building Department, about the newly completed plans for the coffeehouse, Jim headed for his favorite coffee place (well, that is...until his new coffeehouse was built!). He took his coffee outside to walk along the river. Jim was pleased that his new town was beginning to know him and appreciate his efforts to contribute to the town's culture. However, there still seemed to be 'something missing,' he thought. For all these years, he never felt 'alone.' After all, he had his 'work' and that occupied his time and most of his life. Now that he lived in a new town, he felt lonely and wanted to share all these events and 'happenings' with someone beside himself...someone 'special!' His life didn't seem to need anyone else up to this point...he was simply satisfied with just being an architect. So why was he feeling 'lonesome' now? Why did his 'new life' not seem to be so 'fulfilling?' At the age of 52, did he now need a 'relationship' that he had previously tried to avoid? Again he thought, why was he feeling this 'emptiness' now? Looking back, he realized that all those years were without 'someone special...someone close' who could share all the things that made his life 'meaningful.' He thought of Kim...how beautiful she was...the smell of her hair...and that, 'little look' she gave when he passed her way. Could she be the one he was looking for to satisfy this lonely feeling he was experiencing? "No," he thought, "she's just not the one for me." There were many things, he surmised, on which they did not agree. "For instance," he thought: "Remember the time when ...he wanted to go to church and she refused, or when he wanted to go to a bible study and again she refused. She never did understand why he would not sleep with her even after he took time to explain it to her. So what should he do? Go to the local bar to check out whom he might meet there? "No," he thought, "Thats definitely not the answer. I'll just ask God to send someone to me that God knows is 'just right' for me!" So that's what he did. As in all things in which you ask the Holy Spirit for help (since He was sent by God through Jesus to be our 'Helper...our Counselor'), you must understand that, 'His timing' is not necessarily 'our timing.' He knows and prepares the 'right time.' However, you will undoubtedly realize that the 'waiting' is sometimes 'unbearable!' But you always know that when the answer comes, it will be in 'perfect timing!'

As life would have it, the baseball season started at the same time that the construction of the coffeehouse started. The plans were approved by the Building Department and Bill chose the contractor. And who was the contractor? He was the same Christian contractor that Bill worked with to build his own house (which included the space Bill uses for his business). So the days were 'full' and that is an understatement! The baseball League was a total success! The schedule Jim issued was OK'd by all teams. They started right on schedule! Even the snack bar and 'bleachers' were completed and the League Rules signed and OK'd by all teams. 'Josie' was the leader of the snack bar and her husband Barry was the 'Field Maintenance Director!' So the 'announcing' ended up becoming 'Jim's baby' he loved it! He was thus able to meet all the managers and coaches on a personal basis...and even met with most of the players! During one of the practice sessions he attended, there was a young boy who sat at the end of the dugout. He played first base and his fielding ability was pretty good...he got in front of the ball and made the plays. He also had a 'good eye' for the ball when he was hitting (which kids at the age of twelve don't normally have). Most kids this age have to be 'coached...told and shown...over and over.' When one has a player like that, one tends to spend more time with him because he 'quickly absorbs' everything his coach tells him to do. One day, when Jim was observing practice, he witnessed this young boy 'freezing,' that is, 'standing still...motionless,' in the middle of a play! He stood there, not moving, just looking straight ahead, as if his whole world had stopped. The manager, seeing this happening and not knowing exactly what to do, stopped the practice and quickly went over to the young boy. After ten or so minutes, he was fine once again. Jim took him aside and asked him what happened. He said he was sorry for taking the time away from the other guys. He then explained that this sort of thing happened, every once in a while. Jim asked, "Are you all right? Do you need to go to an Emergency Room?" The boy said that he was fine and wanted to finish the practice." Jim said, 'OK' but kept a very close eye on him the rest of the day.

After practice concluded, Jim found out that the young boy's name was 'Jackson Sky.' Jackson introduced Jim to his mother, Amy. "Hello Mrs. Sky," Jim said. "Oh! No need to call me Mrs. Sky...just 'Amy' would be fine." Jim replied, "OK Amy, I need to talk to you about Jackson. It seems that he just 'froze' in one position while he was practicing and frankly, it scared me," said Jim. Amy said, "He's had that condition since he was seven years old. I've taken him to a number of doctor's and none of them could tell me what causes it to happen. I'm a single mother and I have a daughter named Summer. I hope this won't cause Jackson to be kicked off the team!" Jim replied, "No, not yet. I'll talk to his manager and if he continues to have the problem, we'll have a conversation regarding what to do next." Amy responded, "He loves playing and he is a to-tally different boy since you started this league! I can't thank you enough! In fact, his whole life is different...his school grades have improved, he has friends, he even talks with his sister and me! On top of all that, he can't wait to play baseball!" Jim responded, "It's been a real pleasure to start this league! Frankly, I was a bit surprised that there wasn't a baseball league here already." Amy said, "Well, you made many kids and their parents very excited and happy. Now, you must excuse us...we have to get home and start dinner." Jim said, "OK Amy, it's nice meeting you!" She smiled and they went on their way.

Her beauty overwhelms Jim; everything about her is just indescribable. Her looks, the way she handles herself, the way she moves, and her voice was like nothing he ever heard. Wow, this is someone I want to know more Jim thought. His life was so full of architectural business with little time for getting know women and because he lived his life different from other men it wasn't easy to develop relationships without being tempted to change. However, he recognized that life, as he lived it, was changing and he had to move with it or be a very lonely man.

Amy Sky met her husband in High School, and they were married several years later. In fact, she was 32 years old when they recited their wedding vows. At the age of 35, she gave birth to her daughter 'Summer,' a name her husband loved. Two years passed and Jackson was born. A few years later, her husband and father of her children, was killed in Iraq. Amy and her children were sick with grief for several years, but she had two children to take care of, so there wasn't a lot time to grieve. She was raised in a Christian home and her parents were 'the best,' if you asked her. She studied and read the Bible on a regular basis as part of the routine of her life. The cornerstone of her life was her relationship with Jesus Christ and she raised her children the same way. It's been many years since she lost her husband. Now at the age of forty-nine, she recognized she was feeling, 'lonely.' 'Why' she didn't really know...but the feeling was strong and it made her very apprehensive at times. All her life she had that feeling of 'closeness' with someone, but since her parents had passed away and with the loss of her husband, there just wasn't anyone to turn to. She felt a 'hunger' inside but she just didn't really know how to satisfy the emptiness. She always turned to the Lord to help her through the 'challenges' in her life. Now when she prays, she only hears "Trust Me!"

Jim was working on the deck of his new coffeehouse when Bill came along. He had been observing the 'progress' on the Project from time-to-time, but was interested in hearing Jim's perspective of the 'management details,' such as the coordination of the construction 'trades,' the schedule-of-events, etc. After their cordial 'hello's,' Jim told him they were 'on schedule' and the fireplace would start on that following Monday. That excited Bill and he said he wanted to be part of that! "OK then, Monday at 7:00am...and you must bring the coffee!" said Jim. "That's a deal!" said Bill. "By the way, I heard what took place on the ball-field the other day," continued Bill. Jim then filled him in on some of the details: "Ya, I spoke to Jackson's mother. She told me she took Jackson to many different doctors, but they couldn't find out the reason for his 'freezing-up' like he does. Bill, what can you tell me about Amy Sky?" Bill answered with 'gusto,' "You mean besides what a good look-in' gal she is?" Jim somewhat nervously, said, "Ya, that is true." Bill continued, "I can't say much, she's a wonderful Christian mother and very active in the Church." Jim then asked, "In what way?" Bill answered, "Well, on her days off from waiting tables at Joe's Place, you'll most likely find her helping feed the homeless and the poor, or passing out clothes...especially when its cold. I've even seen her walking the streets at night giving blankets to the homeless and she even takes some of them into her home just to keep them warm! I don't think I've ever known anyone who cares more than she does. With her salary at Joe's and a pension from the military, I think she just 'gets by' financially." Jim said, "Her son Jackson is a great kid...I only wish I could help!" Bill replied, "Don't worry, I'm

sure you'll have the opportunity in the near future."

Monday morning came 'bright and early!' The
new stone fireplace was in the process of completion and it was looking great...just as Jim had envisioned. Bill and the contractor were 'working
hard' and it showed! The construction was very
difficult because the foundations for the fireplace
had to be poured 'under-water.' This proved to be
a masterful accomplishment! The contractor's skill
for making such a concerted pour was 'beyond
proficient!' He knew just what to do, even when
one of the forms 'blew-out.' He immediately ad-
dressed the situation, made the 'fix' and continued pouring. If anyone else had been 'running-
the-show,' the entire foundation would have been
lost, resulting in a 'minor disaster!'

What would they call their new coffee place?
Bill said, "Let's call it "The Winless Coffee
Grinders." Someone else said, "Call it 'The Winless Coffee Roasters.'" Another said, "The Wind-
less Coffee Shack." Three good suggestions,
thought Jim. Then he had an idea: "Let's take a
vote from everyone in town! A week from today,
we'll tally the votes and see which one it will be!"
So the town-folk started voting...men, women
and children. Jim was excited because this voting
would give him a better understanding of how

popular the coffee place would be. Soon the week was 'up' and it was time to count the votes. Everyone participating gathered at the coffee-place location to find out the results! Jim noticed that Jackson, Summer and Amy were in attendance. Jim approached them and said, "Its great seeing you here!" Amy said, "We had to find out which name we'll tell our friends to meet us for coffee!" Jim put his arm around Jackson and asked how his team was doing. Jackson said with a big grin on his face "Real good, Mr. Amico...and I'm hitting in the 'cleanup' spot!" Jim said, "Great, Jackson! And if I can be of any assistance, let me know!" Jackson didn't hesitate and said, "Mr. Amico, I need some instruction on hitting the curve-ball and also on 'bunting.'" So Jim suggested, "How about early tomorrow morning now that school is out?" Jackson enthusiastically responded, "That'd be just great! About 8:00am?" Jim confirmed the plan with, "Ok, I'll see you then." Amy came over and thanked Jim for giving Jackson so much attention. "Are you kidding? He's a great kid! You're doing and have done a great job raising the two of them!" was Jim's reply. Amy asked, "Do you mind if I come along? I'm not working tomorrow." Jim said, "No, of course not! I'd like for you to be there and maybe we can all get some lunch after practice." Amy confirmed, "That'd be great."

Summer said she was going shopping with her friends and she would meet them for dinner. "Hey! What about the name?" someone yelled out." Jim remembered, "Yes! OK! We've finished the tally and the new name is? The 'Winless Coffee Shack!'" A big cheer went up from the assembled crowd, as Bill showed up with a cart, which had, hot coffee in it for the adults and soda for the kids! Jim concluded the day's events by saying, "I'd better get started on the design...for the new store-sign! WOW! That even rhymes!"

6

AMY AND JIM

The next day was a bright and sunny with blue skies. Jim had a smile on his face that he hadn't seen for a long time. He met Jackson at his house. Amy came out looking absolutely beautiful. Summer came running by saying, "I'm late I'll see you tonight. Off they went to the ball field. Jim said, "I hope no one is there". Jackson said, "It's too early for anyone to be there". Sure enough the field was empty. So Jim and Jackson worked on the bunting part of what Jackson asked, and Amy sat in the stands watching and thinking that if her husband where a live he would be doing this with her son. Jim pitched and Jackson was listening to very word Jim told him. Each pitch was bunted better, some down the third base line and some down the first base line. Soon the kids in area noticed that Mr. Amico was on the field and giving instruction they all came and gather around to take part in the practice. Jim was now teaching about seven young boys in the art of hitting and they loved every minute. Jim showed them how to be patient and wait on the curve ball. He had them come to the plate one at a time while the other kids played the field. He told them to swing at every pitch because he wanted them to be ready to hit at all times. Not standing there waiting for just the right pitch. He told them that swing at every pitch in practice only not in regular game. However, by swing at every pitch they will begin to feel the pitch more and understand the strike zone better.

Before they knew it, the team which was scheduled to practice showed up and Jim and his boys had to leave, but they put in a good three-hours' of work and Jackson appreciated every moment! Jim then took Amy and Jackson to a restaurant in a town north of Shadow. The restaurant was right near the water and they could see the waves hitting against the shore. Jackson loved it and Amy was pleased to see her son enjoying himself so much. Jackson asked, "Mom, can I walk along the shore?" "OK," she said, "...but be careful!" Jim asked, "Where is Summer today?" Amy said that she went shopping with her girlfriends, but she said to say hello. Jim said, "She's a beautiful young woman...she sure takes after you, you definitely raised her well." Amy responded, "Thank you, they are a hand-full at times." Jim said, "I bet they are! How do you manage work, school for the kids, and 'life' in general?" I taught them that, "...we all have chores to do and as long we do them, we'll have the kind of house that you can bring your friends into any time." Jim continued the conversation by saying, "After we met last week, my partner Bill was concerned about what happened with Jackson and I asked him about you...I hope you don't mind." Amy replied, "No, I don't mind and I must say that I have asked about you also." Jim felt a 'tinge' of excitement, but continued the question: "So tell me more about Jackson, what can be done for him?" Amy (in her humble honesty) said, "I have no idea what to do. I hope and pray to God that it's not serious, 'cause if a cure isn't found, he won't be able to drive when the time comes. I'm at a loss," said Amy. "Maybe I can help," said Jim. "I have a friend who works at a hospital which I helped design a few years ago.

He's a specialist...a Neurologist. Would it be OK if I contacted him about Jackson?" With subdued excitement, Amy said, "Yes! Of course! I understand that you're a believer." Jim replied, "Yes, that's right. And I found out that you are also a believer in Jesus." Amy confirmed his statement and added that she believed that the Holy Spirit led him to come to Shadow."What you've done for this town since you've arrived is outstanding. Not only in my opinion, but many others feel the same way," said Amy. "Have you ever been married?" asked Amy. "No," Jim confessed. "I devoted so much time to my career that I never allowed myself to get close to anybody. I was raised by great parents who taught me how to live and respect myself and all the people around me. So I lived my life in that way. Many of my 'so called friends" made fun of me but I was set in my beliefs and I didn't let it bother me. Sometimes I think that's why women stayed away from me. Since it's my life, I live it my way. I didn't have to answer to anybody except myself and God. I'm sorry, I've probably said more than I should have." Amy said, "No, not at all. It's refreshing to hear a man describe himself in such an open way."

This conversation took place while Jackson was outside watching the waves. When he returned they ordered their lunch. "So you gave up architecture to move to this town" said Amy. "Not really, my intention is to build the coffee shack and do some architecture also, you really can't give up something you loved all your working life". "I guess that's true". "Is it difficult to make such a big and complete change" said Amy. "That is a great question. I wanted so dearly to get out of the city type of life and when my vacation brought me here, I was convinced this is where I wanted to spend the rest of my life right here surrounded by all this beauty". Jim said, looking right in her eyes. Amy agreed with him and thought, what a good man he is and, will she have a chance to know him better. He wanted to ask her about Jackson and what happens to him when he freezes, but thought, Jackson is here, and he could wait to ask that question. "This has been one beautiful day and one of my best day off I ever had" Amy said. "To bad it has to end" "Why does it have to end" said Jim "How about I take you out to dinner tonight" "I don't think I could get a setter at this short notice" said Amy "Try and if you can't we will all go to dinner" "That sounds perfect to me, how about seven tonight" Amy said. "It's a date," Jim said.

Jim went back to his apartment that looked over the Winless river. He felt as excited as a teenager when a girl said 'yes' to him to go on a date! He took a shower and was set for his date with Amy. He hoped that a sitter could be found. He called Bill, "Bill, what are you doing tonight?" He responded, "Just staying home...might watch a movie." Jim asked, "Would you consider watching Jackson and possibly Summer tonight? I have a date with Amy but she doesn't think its possible to get a sitter on such short notice." Bill said, "May and I would be pleased to be your 'backup' as long as it's OK with Amy." "OK," said Jim. "I'll let you know. Thanks a lot, Bill." So Bill immediately called Amy who told him she had found a sitter. Jim called Bill to tell him that he and his wife could go ahead and watch the movie they'd planned. Jim told Bill how grateful he was that Bill had 'volunteered' to be his 'back-up!'

Jim's car found its way to the Sky residence right at 7:00 pm. He was excited and happy to be going on a date with such a beautiful woman. Jackson answered the door with a big "Hello Mr. Amico!" Jim responded exuberantly, "Hi Jackson! We should talk about this 'Mr. Amico' stuff. I think we'll be seeing each other a lot in the future. So instead of calling me Mr. Amico call me, Hawks. My army buddies gave me that name and all my dear friends call me, Hawks. Now I would ask you to get an OK from your mother before we finalize this." Just then Amy appeared and said, "What is it that I must approve?" Jackson said, "Mom, Mr. Amico said I could call him 'Hawks,' if it's OK with you. Well, Mom, is it all right with you?" Jackson pleaded. "Yes, but if we are with other people I still want you to respect Hawks. Do you understand, Jackson?" Amy said. "What about me, Mr. Amico, do I have the same right?" asked Summer. "Sure you do," Jim replied. "Hi Amy...did the sitter show up?" asked Jim. "She did. Let me introduce you to her. Wanda, I would like to you meet Mr. Amico," said Amy. "Hello, Mr. Amico!" said Wanda. Amy grabbed her jacket and said, "Be good kids!" and started for the door. The kids called out "Have a good time!"

They walked to the car and Jim led the way for her. She looked in his eyes and said, "Thank you." Jim opened the door for her as he told her about the reservation he'd made and apologized that this 'special restaurant' was about 45 minutes away. Amy said that that was fine since it would give them some time to talk. "All right then," said Jim, starting the car and the conversation. "What should we talk about?" Amy said, "Do you have any idea how long it's been since I've been on a date?" Jim had no clue, so Amy continued: "Well it's been a number of years!" Jim was quick to respond: "What would you say if I told you that you're one of the most beautiful women I ever have taken on a date!" Amy said modestly, "You're much too kind." Jim changed the subject and said, "It must have been hellish to get the news about your husband being killed in the war." Amy took a moment and said, "You couldn't possibly have any idea. When I saw the two soldiers coming to the door, I almost fainted, but I didn't 'cause I was thinking of the kids.

After the soldiers went back to their car, I couldn't hold back the tears and the kids and I cried for the rest of the day. We talked about what we would miss in Patrick. We prayed for our future and for the kids living without their father. It took countless weeks before we could get through a day without crying. Summer was seven and Jackson was two years old. I didn't think I would ever meet anyone that could compare with Patrick. He was an excellent father and husband. Its true that he wasn't home much of the time because of his military duty, but he made it pretty terrific when he was home. As I said I know there is someone out there for me, but I doubt I'll ever meet him. What about you Jim, did you ever have a woman in your life?" asked Amy? Jim considered what Amy asked him. "I'm a very unusual kind of man. I mentioned that I was raised in an Italian Catholic family. We had a lot of love in my family. My relatives always hugged each other when we would meet. I was raised in a very strict manner. I was taught to respect girls and not to take advantage of them. I was also an introvert. I had very little, if any, self-respect. So consequently I was afraid to step out and do anything. I was bashful around girls. I didn't find myself until I went into the army. I knew nothing about 'life' at seventeen years old. The army gave me the opportunity to grow like I would never have done by living at home. To answer your question: no, I never fell in love or experienced how that would feel. I can tell you this, that you have made me feel something I have never felt before. I don't know what it is yet, but I sure enjoy it. Sitting here with you and sharing things about our lives is something fantastic. I hope you feel the same." Amy responded, "I've never met a man like you. You have qualities about yourself that are relaxing to be around. I am enjoying this conversation."

The restaurant was located on a high hill that overlooked the Winless River. The view was beyond description! They were taken to a table on the outside balcony. Northwestern summers are not the warmest places to be, but with the outside heaters on, it felt warm and cozy. Jim asked Amy, "Is this an acceptable table for you or would you rather be inside?" Amy exclaimed, "Are you kidding me? This is incredible...outstanding...and you make it perfect!"   They looked over the menu...then ordered as Jim graciously recommended. They continued their discussion as they waited for the food to arrive. Jim queried, "What are your plans for the future, Amy? Do you intend to continue waitressing or are you considering something different?" Amy answered, "I know I'm ready for something to change, but this town has very few opportunities." Jim agreed, but then introduced an idea he'd been considering: "That's true, so how about working for me? I'm seriously looking for a manager to run my Coffee House and I think you'd be 'perfect' for the job! What do you say, is that something you might desire to do?" Amy excitedly said, "Jim! That sounds 'tailor-made' for me! I can hardly believe this! Right now, the only thing I can say is...thank you!" Jim was obviously pleased and said, "Amy, you're the only one I had in mind when I realized this need for a manager. I want this person to have their way with this Coffee House (I guess that's a good name for it), but I also want to work closely with them and to understand what they are working on for the place as a benefit to the community. Do you understand what I'm saying"? Amy concurred and said, "Sure, you want to have an essential part in whatever the manager decides to do." Jim acknowledged her understanding and said, "Amy, you're 'right-on-target' and you'll be a big part of our success!"

When dinner concluded, they walked down a brilliantly-lit walkway, found a comfortable bench...sat and talked about everything and nothing and were just happy to be with each other during this incredible evening. As is typical for nights like this in the Northwest, the cold comes in rather abruptly, so staying outside gets somewhat unbearable. Jim removed his jacket and placed it around Amy's shoulders...then led their way to the car. Amy requested that the top to the convertible be closed because the air was becoming somewhat 'frigid.' On the way home, things got a little quiet. Amy said "What are you thinking, Jim?" His response? "I was thinking about you and how I would like to do this again." Amy agreed and said, "I also would love to do this again and let's make it soon." Jim didn't miss a beat: "Would Tuesday night be all right?" Amy didn't hesitate and said, "Yes, about seven would be great!" Jim exuberant ly said, "OK then...we've got another date! So where should we go?" asked Jim. "How about I cook dinner for you?" said Amy. "So your kids can be there too?" Jim asked.

"Yes, of course," replied Amy. "Perfect. I want to spend more time with them as well," Jim said.

Before they knew it, Amy's house was in their view. Jim walked with Amy to the front door and said good night. She looked at him with this loving expression on her face...one that he'd never be able to erase from his mind. She reached up and kissed him and it was so electrifying that Jim didn't know how to respond. "This date was amazing and you are also," said Amy. "Until Tuesday, then." Recovering quickly, Jim said, "Right! Tuesday," said Jim.

"What in God's name is happening to me?" he thought. "I had the time of my life and I couldn't say anything after that kiss! She's definitely someone I want to be around every day of my life. I never felt like this before with any woman. What makes her so different?" She's the most beautiful, kind, grateful, caring...just the best woman he ever knew! So if this is the beginning of love, he was all for it! Amy closed the door behind her and leaned against it and smiled. She hadn't felt like this since she went to high school. Jackson and Summer immediately wanted to know how the date went with Mr. Amico (Hawks). "It was just great and we're having him over for dinner on Tuesday!" said Amy. "Great" said Jackson. "I can't wait!" said Summer. "OK, now off to bed, thank you Wanda!" said Amy as she handed her an envelope. "They were great to be with tonight. I'll see you soon. Good night," said Wanda. Amy was alone in the living room and sat on the couch and was as happy as she could remember. Not only 'happy' but 'excited' at the same time. Could Jim be the man that would fulfill her current dream? Could he be the ONE? Would he love her children? Would working with him destroy their friendship...their new relationship? So many questions,! she said to herself: "I guess we'll just have to pray...and wait to see what our God will do!"

←

←

←

7

THE PURSUIT CONTINUES

A sudden noise, something hitting the window woke Jim from his long sleep. His dream covered most of his life and he felt exhausted and excited at the same time. There are much more pressing matters to deal with on this brand new day. He woke up went down stairs looking around and saw Amy frantically working in his kitchen making coffee. He was surprised to see her there after the day she had yesterday. She said, "I just wanted to get you going early this morning." It was then he remembered Summer was still missing. "Thank you sweetheart, I need you to keep me alert." He drank his coffee, got fully dressed and started out the door. Amy stopped him and gave him a bag full of food and some cold drinks and of course a big hug and kiss that he would remember for a long time. She told him that she filled his truck with gas as he pulled open the door. He yelled thanks as he pulled away. He turned his thoughts to Summer; it's been two days since she was last seen.

He was more hopeful because they found the other three girls, but he knew that time was not on his side. He passed by Bill's house and yelled out the window for him. He came out the door, dressed and ready to go; he also had a bag. It looked like May had done the same thing for Bill that Amy had done. Jim started driving up the same road they took when they first started their search. He said, "Lets think this through. Where do you think this crap-head would take her?" Bill said, "The Highway Patrol went all through the area where we found the other girls but they didn't find any other clues." Jim suppositions, "We have to start thinking the way the kidnapper would. Let's see, if you had beautiful girl like Summer, where would you take her?" Bill said, "Remember...he'd want the most pleasure he could get before his quick get-away." Jim replied, "Right! He most likely has found or has some place hidden away where he could have shelter and some place comfortable." Bill pointed out that there were several places like that around the lake. Jim replied, "Good idea!" The town of Shadow was famous for the river that runs its way through it. However, few know about the many lakes that surround the town. The residents around the lakes are very wealthy and have some of the most expensive homes in the area. Most of these homes are not occupied all year round. Their residents live somewhere else and come back at certain times of the year. So if the kidnapper knew which houses were vacant, he could stay and enjoy himself for as long as he wanted. Because the homes were not very close to each other, an investigation of this magnitude would not be easy. Filled with new-found energy, they decided to start asking questions of those residents who did live there all year-round. A few said they thought they had seen a black man with a young girl in the back of his car. They didn't give much thought to it until the question was now being asked. Jim just kept driving and asking questions of anyone who'd give them their time. Nothing came up, so after several hours, Jim and Bill stopped to eat their bag lunches and have some coffee. "Maybe you should take me home and let me get my own truck," said Bill. "That way, we could look in different areas and cover more ground." So off they went, back to Bill's house. Jim said, "I'll be at the north side of the lake and Bill, you work the south side. I've got a set of walkie-talkies in the back; you can take one of those. Check-in every fifteen minutes," Bill responded, "You got it Jim! Let's remember to keep the Highway Patrol up-to-date." Jim said, "Right again, Bill! And let's also remember that he dropped the original truck, so he must've stolen another car or truck. Bill! Check again with the Highway Patrol to see if they have any notices of stolen vehicles." Bill said that the last time he checked, the Highway Patrol had no news of any stolen vehicles; but they'd 'stay alert' and contact both of us immediately if any reports came in.

←

8

SUMMER ASSAULTED

When Summer woke up, she looked around the room she was in. The room was dark and the curtains were pulled tight so little light could come in. The room had furniture that was new and modern also expensive. She tried to move her arms and could not because they were tied to the headboard and her legs were also tied to the bed's footboard. She had no clothes on and was very cold with legs spread open she was totally exposed. The man that took her was outside the room; she could hear him moving around. She re-members being drugged not knowing how she got here. She thought about her friends what, happened to them she wondered. She never gave away her innocents away and she didn't want to have this man steal it from her. She prayed to the Lord and cried, she heard a voice it was low and faint and it said, "I am with you." She heard a noise at the door she turned her head to the right and the door opened. An older man came in and looked at her, first at her face and then down to her breast and down further. She was scared than she has ever been in her life. He started taking off his clothes. Soon he was naked has she was and over to the right side of the bed. She didn't want to remember what happened next. The pain was like nothing she had ever felt in her life. When he stopped she knew her days of being a virgin were over. She cried uncontrollable. He got dressed and left the room without saying a word. This act happened several times throughout the day.

Amy made breakfast for Jackson and started watching the news. Jackson was sad and didn't know what to do. Amy said, "I think you should go to the game today. Get your mind off your sister; there are good men looking for her. She is going to be fine the Lord will watch over her." Jackson said, "That's easier said." " I know sweetheart." So Jackson took off with his friends and went to play baseball.

The day was sunny with a few clouds against a blue sky. Jackson's sister was on his mind and he just couldn't stop thinking about her. He was the clean-up hitter for the team and his team-mates and the fans were all counting on him to do his job. He focused on his position in the field and soon the inning was over. He trotted to the dugout and waited for his turn to bat. The first hitter got on with a single up the middle, and the next batter hit another single to the right side of the infield. The number three hitter made the first out with a pop-up to left field. Jackson was walking to the batter's box, swinging his bat as always...but all of a sudden, he 'froze!' The umpire was aware that Jackson might have one of his spells, so the game was halted and 'time-out' was called. Jackson's manager came over to him and said to the others, "We'll just let him be for a minute." After about fifteen minutes, he came out it. He emphatically told his manager that he had to get to Jim Amico! "Why is it so important to see Jim right now?" asked his manager. "Because I know where my sister is! he exclaimed. "I got a vision while I was frozen, so I need to get to Jim as soon as possible!" There happened to be a Highway Patrol officer present because his son was playing in the game. He took Jackson to the local station and asked him where his sister was and he said, "I'll tell you at the same time I tell Jim Amico!" So they called Jackson's house and talked to Amy. Jackson got on the phone with his mother and told her what happened. She called Jim on his cell phone and let him speak with Jackson. "Jackson! Where is she?" asked Jim. "Do you know where Bob Hampton lives? It's a large house on the North side of the lake. It's different because it has a big skylight over the entrance!" shouted Jackson. Jim said, "I think I know where it is and I'm going there right now!" The Highway Patrol said they'd send a few cars out there and that Jim should wait for them. There was no sound from Jim. 'Time' was all-important, and 'waiting' was not what Jim wanted to do! The Highway Patrol called Bill and told him what happened. Bill headed for the Hampton's house as fast as his truck could take him! Jim was there first and was vigilantly scanning the house and yard-area when Bill came quietly up to him! "I'm going around back, Bill, Jim whispered. "You take the side-door and try not to spook him!" Jim crawled around the back and was being as 'quiet' as possible. Bill made his way discreetly to the side-door.

Jim looked into the big window on the back of the house and watched as a 'white' man who was about sixty years old, was making a sandwich at the kitchen counter. Bill silently was able to open the side door and stepped inside the house. Jim went around the side where Bill was and entered the house also. They didn't say a word and didn't see any gun (as the girls said he had when he first approached them at the wooded campsite). So, do they jump him with brute force or wait for the Highway Patrol? Jim decided to just jump him and take him down! Jim turned the knob of the door and rushed in! The old man was startled and froze! Jim punched him as hard as he could...right in the nose! He went down to the floor and Jim jumped on top of him and called out to Bill who came running in and helped him tie-up the old man! Jim jumped to his feet to look for Summer. He rushed upstairs, quickly checking each room as he went. One room had the door ajar and, sure enough, she was there, naked and cold! He took a sheet and put it over her as he untied her arms and legs. He took her in his arms and held her tight as she sobbed uncontrollably! Jim whispered softly, "I'm so sorry, you sweet little girl, that you had to go through this nightmare. You are safe now Summer...I'll find your clothes and take you home." She didn't say a word as he found her pants and shirt with her underclothes. She was dressed now and still clinging to Jim. He picked her up and put her in his truck just as the Highway Patrol came rolling up. Bill brought the kidnapper out and handed him over to the Patrol officers. Jim thanked Bill for all his help, then started his truck and headed home with his beautiful little girl. Bill left the scene in his truck and headed back to his home. Jim was so excited Summer was alive, although he knew she must've gone through something very horrific! She looked at him and said, "I knew you would find me!" Jim said, "It wasn't me that found you...it was your brother Jackson. He had one of his 'spells' and had a vision of you in the Hampton's house. Bill and I were just the ones out here looking for you. So it was your brother...and God who gave him the vision! That's who you should thank." "Maybe so, but it was you and Bill who were out there looking for me!" she said. Summer was cold even with Jim's arms around her. "How are the other girls?" she asked. "They're O.K. We picked them up yesterday and they are in good condition. Summer, first I'm going to take you home to your mom and brother...then we'll take you to the hospital to check you out, but..." Summer interrupted and said, "OK Jim, but just stay with me!" Jim reassured her and said, "You know I will!"

←

←

9

VIOLATED

Jim pulled up the driveway and her mom came running out to greet her along with her brother. Hug's and kiss came flowing to her from everyone. Friends and neighbors who came when the word got out that she is found.   Jim said, "I wanted to bring her here so you all could welcome her home, but she must go to the hospital for her exam and, Jim stopped short of saying rape kit. Amy got in the back seat, so lets get this over with so she can take a shower and get comfortable." At the way to the hospital Jim looked over to her and said, "Did he rape you sweetheart, " she nodded yes with her head down on her chest. "This will be easy just let the detective and the nurse do the exam and fellow their instructions and I'll get you right back home as soon they are done. Your mom will be there to help you so don't be frighten. I'll be just outside your door."

She had been violated more than once and various wounds that were rape-related were found on her body. She was in tears throughout most of the exam and so was her mother. After the exam, they took her home and Jim wondered...how do we act toward her? Do we ask her about what happened or do we say nothing until she wants to talk? The latter option was best by far. When they arrived home, she didn't say a word. She ran up to her room and they heard the shower start to run. Amy was so shaken that she went to the sofa put her head in her hands and cried. Jim went over to her and put his arm around her and she rested her head on his chest. "What do I do now?" she cried and wondered. Jim spoke softly and said, "We just love her and pray for her...and do everything we can to make sure she comes out of this thing with a sense of self worth."

The night passed quietly and the morning was bright sunny and warm. Jim came in the door around eight a.m., Amy greeted him with a kiss. He asked about Summer. Amy said, "We talked a little last night she was still shaken and very tired.

She slept and I covered her up and came down-stairs. I heard her cry out a few times during the night but went back to sleep quickly. Jim I'm so pleased that it was you who found her I wouldn't want anyone else to see her, being naked as she was." Jim said, "I put a sheet on her as fast as I could, " "I know she told me." Amy I would like to start a prayer group for Summer. At first it will be just us and some close friends like Bill and May. Then we could expand it to a wider group in the future." "Good, Jim I think that is what God would want." He looked up and Summer is standing in front of them. "I heard you about the prayer group and I think I want that also. I want to tell you something, what I went through was horrible and I will have nightmares for a long time. Here is something that you can't imagine, the Lord held me in his arms, especially when that guy was raping me. He comforted me and said that my life will not be ruined; He will bless me to be-come the woman He intended me to be. He said it was up to me as how my life will be, will I be-come a victim or will I hold my head up and fol-low His lead, and I choose to follow Him where ever He leads me." Amy and Jim put their arms around her and rejoiced that our God's love was so powerful that He took a horrific situation and turned it into praise for His glory. "Oh another thing when are you two getting married, don't you think its time." Jim and Amy knew that this reaction was different then what they expected. The beauty of God's grace canceled out, the grief that we are feeling. They hoped that the future would be eased by Summer 's ability to see this differently, then the world will see it.

Looking over the last week, Jim could see a change taking place in this modest town. A new understanding of love arose between friends and neighbors. A town became more watchful over their own and other children...a town wanted to be 'closer' so they could shelter their beliefs and share with others without fear. They understood that in order to avoid anything like this happening again, they must tie themselves together with a bond so strong that no one would attempt to do something in this manner ever again.

Summer remained in her room for several days trying to lose the lingering thoughts of what she had experienced. She was violated...and those thoughts and feelings, with the Grace of her God and the help of the Holy Spirit, would leave her one day and she hoped and prayed that, 'one day' would be soon! She kept praying and soon she gave it all to the Lord. She started to go out of the house for short walks and to absorb the beauty that God had made. She was becoming the woman God had intended her to be.

The town, on the other hand, was 'shaken to the core.' Four of their teenagers had been kidnapped, so they watched their kids more closely than ever before. They counted on neighbors to look out for the kids in town. They were becoming more involved in their kids' school and other activities.

←

10

Amy Goes To Work

Life continues to happen no matter the situation. So the town of Shadow began to come back to life after a sad and terrifying journey. The Coffee Shack was open and business was doing great. The Baseball League was coming to the end of its season with the playoffs just around the corner. It was good to focus on something other than the kidnapping and the up-coming trial. Jim's town does not have the capability or the facilities to host a trial of this magnitude. So the County Court House would be the site of jurisdiction. The trial was months-away and the town wanted to put this event behind them as quickly as they could.

Amy's management of the Coffee Shack was just starting, but one could begin to see her influence in the decor of the building's interior. The large deck was full of traffic just the way Jim had envisioned. People would come and sit for a period of time, watching the river go rolling by. Early morning coffee groups would gather while most of the other coffee drinkers were apparently still sleeping, or perhaps trying to 'muster the energy' to start their new day. Amy and Bill were the only employees, but something needed to be done because the load was too much for just the two of them. So through 'word-of-mouth,' they had many job applications from which to choose.

Four of the fourteen baseball teams made it into the playoffs. The games would be played on Friday night and Saturday...then the winners of these games would play each other the following Saturday. Jackson's team had made the playoff's, which made Amy and Summer very happy and excited to see Jackson playing.

Summer was progressing and dealing with 'life' after her traumatic experience. She decided to go to summer school to pick up some extra credits, but she changed her mind and just wanted to watch her brother play in the playoffs. She didn't want to focus on what had transpired. She wanted to look forward to the life that God had planned for her. She continued to heal from the physical injuries she had incurred and her Doctors said she hadn't sustained any long lasting effects that would prevent her from having children. All that was extremely good to hear, but Jim and Amy were more concerned about her mental condition. The doctor said, "You live with her, Amy...how does she seem to you?" Amy answered, "She looks and acts normal, but is that 'normal' for someone who's been through what she has? What is 'normal' to you?" Doctor Howard responded, "She should see a counselor...that would go a long way toward helping her cope with the future." Summer said, "No, I don't need a counselor, I have Jesus and He's more than enough.

Summer continued to show her strength in overcoming the terrible things she'd been through on that outing in the woods. Jim had become the 'shoulder' she could lean on. They went on walks and talked together many times and on one of their walks, he asked her, "Did this kidnapper say anything to you or blurb something out?" She surprised herself and remembered, "Yeah, one time. He said, 'this is for my son.'" Jim exclaimed, "Wow! That's a strange thing to say! Do you know any boys in town that you've had some words with or an argument with in recent days?" She responded, "No, there are no boys that would have any reason for doing something this bad." Jim put that in the back of his mind. Sometime in the future, those few words could mean a great deal.

Summer has told Jim that when she feels like she's 'adjusting favorably' and becoming more 'in control,' there's always something or someone who takes her back into, that 'dark place' she's trying to crawl out from under. In this case, it happened to be the detectives from the Shadow Police Department, detectives Joan Blank and Ralph Roundtree. "We just have a few more questions for Summer, if you don't mind," was their opening comment when Amy opened the door. Seeing them hold their badges up for her to see, Amy would invite them in and called for Summer. They'd introduce themselves again and begin to ask questions about the incident that Summer experienced. The questions were routine and only accomplished one thing: they brought back into focus the entire horrifying act for both Summer and her mother. When the question-and-answer session was over and the tears were wiped away (and 'apologies' were given), the detectives left and Amy and Summer held each other for a few minutes. Summer went back to her room and once again began the process of pushing away the memories that tore her apart on the inside.

11

Hear The Holy spirit

Sunday was full of anticipation, its time to join with friends and neighbors and go to the church of their choice. Uplifting as this day is, it is also a time of healing for individuals and the town as a whole. It's odd that in this area of the state, the census recorded the lowest attendance of church goers. It's also odd because there are several churches in this town and they are all doing well, but most likely, not as well as they would like. However, their doors stay open. The church Jim and the Sky family attend is a nondenominational Christian Church. It has approximately two hundred and fifty people attending on a weekly basis.

The pastor is a mature, sixty-year-old man in love with the God he preaches about.

Jim remembers the night that Bill introduced him to Jesus Christ. Bill showed him a 'Jesus' he had never seen before. He felt love from God and he, in return, loved Him back. For the first time in his life, Jim considered asking a woman to spend the rest of her life with him! Once he realized how much he's loved by the God who created him (and finally understood what 'love' really is)...it became easy for him to love someone else. Amy Sky is becoming more important to him each day that goes by. After going through that horrible event with Summer, Amy and Jim have become closer and find that their days are intertwined, not only because of the Coffee Shack, it seems now they do everything together. So he sits in Church asking God for guidance and the words to say that tell Amy how he feels.

Soon the singing stopped and the pastor began his message for the week. Jim could never understand why pastors think a message is the best way to 'end' a Church service, when it should be the 'beginning' of a week of service to God as instructed in the Scriptures. It seemed to Jim that the reason for Church is to praise, give thanks and honor to God. Why is a message so important? Jim understood that reading and studying the word is significant, but 'Church' is a time for worship...prayer...thanksgiving for all of God's wonderful 'gifts.'

The pastor began his sermon by saying, "We look at the world and we see the darkness that surrounds us and wonder what will happen to us. Could that be the problem? Are we all looking at the wrong things? We're focused on 'us' and what may become of 'us' if the world continues on the path that it is taking. Jim grasped that message and thought, "We should take our eyes off the world and ourselves, then put our focus on the One who has given us 'everything' which makes up all facets of this miraculous world! That's right! And His name is 'Jesus!' We need to take the time to look at and study 'the One' who is all-beautiful, all-loving, all-giving, and the only wise One!" Jim surmised that our problems would take on 'new meaning' if we would see the answers to all the world's problems...in Jesus! We'd see the answers to all our problems. In Him, there is joy, peace, kindness, and the correct response to all things. Jesus accomplished His mission in 'absolute obe-dience' to the 'will' of His Father; that is, rising from the grave (just as He told His disciples he would) three days after He suffered and died on the cross for our sins. He became the 'Sacrificial Lamb'...the substitute...the atonement (since the only atonement for sin is a 'blood sacrifice'). After His followers (about 500 of them) got over the initial 'astonishment' of what Jesus had done, they began to wonder what would happen next. They asked Him if He would now establish His Kingdom throughout all Israel, but He said that the Father was the only One with that authority, and that He must go to the Father so that the Father could send them a 'helper, a comforter' that would tell them much more about Him and the Triune God. He told them that when they received the Spirit, they would have the power, the authority, to go into all the world with the 'Good News' (which is the meaning of the word 'Gospel'). However, some of us have not allowed this 'gift' to be received. Why have we not understood what Jesus was saying? Is it because, in 'living,' we have listened to someone who gave us the wrong information...or was it our parents who received this information and passed it on to us?

There's a story that the author would like to tell you. It's an old story and most likely you might have heard it before. If so, bear with me. It's about a farmer who was doing his farming-thing on his tractor. One day, while plowing his field, he came across an egg lying on the ground. It was a large egg, not like a chicken's egg...and he didn't know what to do with it. So he put it in his pocket and when he returned to the farm, he placed it in the chicken coop. So happens that this one hen took it as her own and sat on it until it hatched. So this little one was raised like a chicken, he did things that chickens do. He pecked on the ground like other chickens and lived a chicken's kind of life. Well, one day this eagle was flying around and happened to look down and notice this baby eagle walking around this chicken coop. So he flew down to the chicken coop and talked to the baby eagle and said, "What are you doing here?" The baby eagle said "What do you mean? I'm a chicken...that's why I'm here." The eagle said "No you're not! You're an eagle!" The baby eagle said, "You're nuts! I've been a chicken all my life...I can't be an eagle." So the eagle took him to the top of great hill nearby. He said, "Look at the eagles...you are one of them! You are not a chicken!" "You're wrong," said the baby eagle. "I can't fly like that." That's when the eagle pushed the baby eagle off the great hill and he began to fall...until he started to flap his wings! Then he felt himself 'soar' just like the other eagles...exactly as the eagle had said.

Why is this story important? It's important because the story of the baby eagle is <u>our</u> story. The story of the baby eagle is the story of <u>our</u> lives. Each of us is different and our life experiences are divergent. We come from varying lives and each of us sees things in contrasting views.

Our lives have led us in different directions. We were taught things by people we loved and respected. People who learn the bible by those who 'thought' they knew what the Bible was saying...perhaps were misinterpreting what the Bible is really teaching. Sometimes we don't consider that these interpretations could be erroneous because that would diminish our confidence and respect for the ones we love. It's important that one listens closely and confirms the teaching for oneself. Be vigilant! Never take anything that someone says about the Word without checking it out for yourself. The subject of the Holy Spirit is too important for you to misinterpret Him without getting into the Word for yourself. Should you have questions, then by all means, 'ask!' Do it in a group so not one person is offering their opinion without having a discussion.

When we come to Jesus, He 'intertwines' our lives together with His. So we should look at life the way He wants us to see it, because He 'created' our very lives. That is why the Holy Spirit inspired the writing of the Bible. In order for us to experience life the way Our Lord intended, we must understand who we are in Christ. We cannot achieve this until the Holy Spirit dominates our thoughts and our actions. Listen to what Jesus said in John 14:16-21, "I will pray to the Father and He will give you another [Helper, Com-forter] Counselor, I will not leave you as orphans, I will come to you." Reading the entire passage will give you much more insight! The Holy Spirit is an essential part of knowing who we are in Christ. You may be thinking, "What is the pastor trying to communicate when he talks about '...who we are in Christ'?" Unless we process the knowledge of what was accomplished on the cross, we will never be able to live the victorious life that Jesus wants for all his beloved.

The lesson, the 'teaching,' inherent in the story of the farmer and the eagle is to remind us all that we have 'matured' with many incompatible teachings; some are good and some, not so good. Because of such teachings, we have devel-oped some erroneous beliefs...beliefs that have shaped our way of seeing the Gospels. Some of you may have been told that the Holy Spirit is someone that should not be embraced and should be kept silent. The TRUTH is: The Holy Spirit is the third person of the Holy Trinity which is made up of the Father, His only begotten Son Jesus the Christ, and the Holy Spirit. If we really pay attention to the words we read in the Bible, we'll see how God the Father and Jesus Christ His Son, value this gift of the Holy Spirit. The Holy Spirit is so important and valuable that when we become followers of Jesus and ask Him to be part of our lives, we become a 'temple' where the Holy Spirit resides.

We need to pause here and reflect on the Bible's teaching (John 14:16-21) because we need to get acquainted with the person of the Holy Spirit. Prepare yourself, because this journey will be life changing! You'll begin to see the 'true essence' of the Gospel of Jesus Christ. You will be released to go with God the Father, Jesus Christ His Son and with the Precious Holy Spirit

Jim, Amy, Summer, and Jackson were leaving the Church when Bill and May joined them. "What did you think of the service?" asked Bill. "It sure was different," Jim said. "This series is going to be filled with very 'unconventional' messages from our pastor," Bill said. "I was speculating as to how we should approach the subject." Jim then asked Bill, "What do you mean?" Bill responded, "Well, I've been a Christian for many years and I still don't know that much about the Holy Spirit. Can we get together and study this subject as a group and maybe we can learn from each other?" Amy chimed in with, "That's a great idea! You all could come to our house on Tuesday night and I'll make dinner, then we'll have the Bible-study right after we eat!" May concurred and said, "That'll be great! Oh! Beforehand, let's do some studying on the subject and come to the meeting with some understanding of the person of the Holy Spirit. And Amy, I'll call you to help with the preparations."

The person of the Holy Spirit has been a difficult topic for Christians to understand or comprehend. Reasons have varied from fear, misunderstanding, to almost a dislike for the Holy Spirit, based on their misinterpretation of the concept of a 'spiritual language,' sometimes called 'tongues.' Why? God the Father and His Beloved Son made it clear that this was a 'gift' from above...necessary for the provision of the 'Saints' who are also called 'Believers.' There's one thing our enemy knows: he's failed in his mission if we listen to and act according to what God says. So if the Father and His Son want His Church to have a gift from above, it most likely is something of great power and authority. So the 'evil one' set out to undermine the Holy Spirit. He did it very slowly, until he had pastors, priests, Bible teachers and thus their congregations, staying away from the 'person' of the Holy Spirit. However, the pastor of Jim's newly-found Church is willing to take on the subject of the Holy Spirit and exhibits 'no fear' of the subject-matter!

←

12

INTRODUCTION TO HOLY SPIRIT

The sky was bright, with puffy white clouds floating along in the expanse of blue. It was Tuesday, a day when the Coffee Shack is visited by groups that use the Shack for their Bible studies. It usually means a great deal of business will take place. That means Amy will be painfully busy with very little time to get away and prepare for tonight's dinner with Bill and May. As soon as the thought came to her mind, who comes in but May herself! "It's obvious that you're 'really busy' today and I bet you don't have time to prepare a dinner for us tonight, am I right?" said May. "You read my mind," said Amy. "Then let me help! I'll do the shopping and start the prep for tonight so when you get home you won't have do it all," said May. "I can't put you out like that, May!" Amy said. "Don't be silly...I have nothing to do until our meeting tonight, so this is perfect for me!" May insisted. "What a relief, May...thank you!" said Amy who was very grateful she had friends like May. She then refocused her attention on the day's events. A few major deliveries came on Tuesdays, one being the coffee and the other the milk delivery.

After putting it all in proper perspective, Amy took a break and stepped-out onto the deck for a little breather. She took a seat and was watching the river when a man sat next to her. She looked around and he said, "Hi! I'm Ryan. We went to high school together. Haven't seen you for...God I can't remember when!" Amy got up and they hugged and both sat back down. "So tell me Amy, how have you been?" asked Ryan. "I'm good. I run this place for my friend. So, what brings you to these parts? I heard you live in California," said Amy." I just started to think about the old days," replied Ryan. "I wanted to come back to see how things turned out for the ones I care about. I heard what happened to Summer and wanted to come and be by your side through what I believe to be some terrifying weeks. However, life had something else in mind, like a car accident that almost left me in a wheel-chair for the rest of my life. Amy, you know me. When I'm faced with a difficult time, I have to 'fight' my way through until I get to the other side...and I did! I have very few side-effects from the accident; today, I feel like a million dollars! Seeing you makes it even better." Said, Ryan. "We can thank God you're doing so well, Ryan! But right now, I have to get back to work," said Amy. "I understand, so can I take you out to dinner?" asked Ryan. "I don't think that would be appropriate. I'm seeing someone," said Amy. "I'll be in town for a few weeks...maybe lunch sometime?" said Ryan.

Amy's day was soon behind her, but not before a picture of the past was set in her mind. She remembered Ryan back in her high school days and how different he was compared with her impression of him during today's visit. He hung around people that she didn't want anything to do with. He was always incompatible with her friends and never seemed that interested in her, which was fine with her. So why did he feel it necessary to drive up here from California to visit? It just seemed strange to her.

As the door closed to the Coffee Shack, Amy began to think about her day and how glad she was that it was over. She walked to her car thinking about the dinner and Bible study that would soon be taking place in her home. She thought about Jim and felt safe and loved. When she arrived home, she found Summer and May preparing dinner and she immediately volunteered her help. May said, "You can relax and get comfortable...we'll serve dinner in short time." Amy was excited that everything was done; she was so exhausted after a long day at the Coffee Shack. So she took May's advice: took off her shoes...put on her slippers and went into the living room to relax. Jim gave her a kiss and Jackson said, "Hi mom!" Bill said, "It must be good to be home after a long day." Amy smiled and said, "You can say that again!" She thought of Ryan again and why he'd 'shown up' after such a long time. What was he looking to do in Shadow? They were never even friends during high school. Why did he keep track of her, even knowing about Summer's kidnapping? She couldn't even remember his last name. They hadn't talked to each other since he asked her to the prom, and she had declined.

Before long, dinner was served and God's Blessings were asked over the food. Scintillating conversations occurred and before they knew it, dinner was over. May stated, "It seems like more time is always spent in the 'preparation' and 'cooking' of a meal...then in just a few minutes, it's all over!" Jim said, "Except for the clean-up, which Bill and I (and yes, Jackson...you can help too) will be doing tonight."

After the clean-up was complete, it was time for the Bible-study. Everyone was eager to start because it seemed like they all had put in some work on the subject since the Sunday service. The room they were in was large and pleasant; a large fireplace was centered on one wall with two cozy, restful couches on each side...big enough to hold everyone. Centered at the end of the two couches was a comfortable, over-stuffed chair. Jim sat in that chair and said, "Bill, I'll give up this chair if you want to lead the group tonight." "No," said Bill. "I don't have a full-understanding about our subject." Everyone took time to settle down and get comfortable. Jim started with a question, "Has anyone read about the Holy Spirit since the pastor spoke on Sunday?" Summer responded first and said, "I did Jim, and I don't really get it. The Holy Spirit is the third person of the Triune Godhead and is given to us when we become a Christian. What more is there to know?" Jim then asked, "Would anyone else like to expand on

Summer's observation?" Amy said, "It's my under-standing that, as Christians, we have become the 'temple' of the Holy Spirit." Bill stated, "...and I understand that receiving the Holy Spirit is not necessary for salvation." Jim took the 'leadership role' and said, "All of that is true. However, fur-ther explanation is needed for each of these ob-servations. We all know that we must be 'born again.' What did Jesus say to Nicodemus when he came to Him? Jesus knew that Nicodemus was giving Him praise to get on His 'good side' as men like Nicodemus do. But Jesus came right to the point without hesitation and said, 'Most certainly, I tell you, unless one is born anew, he cannot see the Kingdom of God.' So here we see Jesus telling him that he is 'dead' in his sin and he must be 'born again' for him to see God's Kingdom. Before we became 'Christian,' we too were 'dead' be-cause of our sin; but, we are now 'born again.' What part of us was born again?" Jackson an-swered and said, "Our spirit was born again." Jim answered, "That's correct! Our spirit was born again. The reason this is so important is that it reminds us how important our spirit is to God. If our spirit is important to God, how do you think He feels about the Holy Spirit? Remember, we re-ceive the Holy Spirit when we receive our 'salva-tion.' And we receive our 'salvation' when we accept Jesus as our Lord and Savior. That's when we become the 'temple' of the Holy Spirit because the Holy Spirit came inside of us. Like drinking a glass of water...the water is inside of us. Is that it, is there anything else? Let's listen to what Jesus said in John 16:7-33:

John 16:7-33

7 Nevertheless I tell you the truth: It is to your advantage that I go away, for if I don't go away, the Counselor won't come to you. But if I go, I will send him to you.

8 When he has come, he will convict the world about sin, about righteousness, and about judgment;

9 about sin, because they don't believe in me;

10 about righteousness, because I am going to my Father, and you won't see me anymore;

11 about judgment, because the prince of this world has been judged.

12 "I have yet many things to tell you, but you can't bear them now.

13 However when he, the Spirit of truth, has come, he will guide you into all truth, for he will not speak from himself; but whatever he hears, he will speak. He will declare to you things that are coming.

1 4 He will glorify me, for he will take from what is mine, and will declare it to you.

1 5 All things whatever the Father has are mine; therefore I said that he takes of mine, and will declare it to you.

1 6 A little while, and you will not see me. Again a little while, and you will see me."

17 Some of his disciples therefore said to one another, "What is this that he says to us, 'A little while, and you won't see me, and again a little while, and you will see me;' and, 'Because I go to the Father?' "

18 They said therefore, "What is this that he says, 'A little while?' We don't know what he is saying."

19 Therefore Jesus perceived that they wanted to ask him, and he said to them, "Do you inquire among yourselves concerning this, that I said, 'A little while, and you won't see me, and again a little while, and you will see me?'

20 Most certainly I tell you, that you will weep and lament, but the world will rejoice. You will be sorrowful, but your sorrow will be turned into joy.

2 1 A woman, when she gives birth, has sorrow, because her time has come. But when she has delivered the child, she doesn't remember the anguish any more, for the joy that a human being is born into the world.

22 Therefore you now have sorrow, but I will see you again, and your heart will rejoice, and no one will take your joy away from you.

23 "In that day you will ask me no questions. Most certainly I tell you, whatever you may ask of the Father in my name, he will give it to you.

24 Until now, you have asked nothing in my name. Ask, and you will receive, that your joy may be made full.

25 I have spoken these things to you in figures of speech. But the time is coming when I will no more speak to you in figures of speech, but will tell you plainly about the Father.

26 On that day you will ask in my name; and I don't say to you, that I will pray to the Father for you,

27 for the Father himself loves you, because you have loved me, and have believed that I came forth from God.

28 I came out from the Father, and have come into the world. Again, I leave the world, and go to the Father."

29 His disciples said to him, "Behold, now you speak plainly, and speak no figures of speech.

30 Now we know that you know all things, and don't need for anyone to question you. By this we believe that you came forth from God."

31 Jesus answered them, "Do you now be-lieve?

3 2 Behold, the time is coming, yes, and has now come, that you will be scattered, everyone to his own place, and you will leave me alone. Yet I am not alone, because the Father is with me.

3 3 I have told you these things, that in me you may have peace. In the world you have op-pression; but cheer up! I have overcome the world."

So who is this 'Counselor' that Jesus speaks of in this portion of scripture? It is none other than the Holy Spirit. In this scripture, Jesus is telling us of the importance of the Holy Spirit. He is saying to us that He and the Father want us to have this Counselor or 'Helper'...the Spirit of truth. What-ever translation you read, it means the Holy Spirit. He will convict the world of sin, and that means he will convict the world of the only sin...that of not believing in the Son of God, who is 'The One' who takes away the sin of the world and His Name is Jesus Christ. He will convict the Believers of Righteousness, this means that the believers are no longer in sin; they have right-standing with God. Sin does not impact their lives any longer. He also will judge the 'prince' of this world, which is the devil...the 'evil one.'

So we can see that the Holy Spirit will show to the believers, the completed work of Jesus Christ. He shows that, because of Jesus, we have right-standing with God the Father. He shows us that Jesus paid the price entirely for our sins. He shows us that, because of Jesus, we are now and forever Children of the Living God. We find ourselves trying to be good, trying not to sin, trying to live a life worthy of Jesus. We must stop all of that 'trying' because our Savior has done it all! We ourselves cannot do anything to achieve salvation! What makes us think we can do anything to take salvation away? WE CAN'T... except if we 'blaspheme' the Holy Spirit, which means 'denying' the existence of the Holy Spirit or speaking irreverently about Him. We must learn to 'rest

in the 'finished work' of Jesus Christ! Jesus gave up His life so that we can 'truly live!' What makes us think we can do anything pleasing for God? The Word says that our best deeds are like 'filthy rags.' So we 'try' to live a good life, thinking that we can achieve anything on our own, but we are fooling ourselves. Jesus is all that matters! He did it all for us...now we must 'rest' in Him. The only way we can be pleasing to the Father is to lift up His Son! Jesus is the One who made us right-standing with God, not us..."lest we should boast!" Jesus was made to be at the right-hand of

God our Father. Jesus made us children of the most-high God...this was not our doing. It is Jesus alone that bore our sins on the cross...for us! So why are we trying to replace Him by doing 'good works' by ourselves? We say, "We're not trying to replace Him." Yes we are...every time we try to be 'good' to achieve a better 'standing' with the Father; that's exactly what we are trying to do. Instead, we must establish a 'kinship' with Christ which consists of doing the 'will' of God. And what is it to do the 'will' of God? There is but one answer: Behold the Man...the Man Jesus! We must 'be' like Jesus...follow in His footsteps, just as He lived on this Earth! We are to emulate 'The Savior,' the Lover of our soul. The Perfect One.

So where did these words about Jesus come from? They came through the power of the Holy Spirit. What did Jesus say? "He [meaning the Holy Spirit] will tell you all about Me [Jesus]." That's the power of the Holy Spirit that the world can not receive because they do not 'know' Him and therefore cannot 'believe' in Him. What about us? Do we truly 'know' Him? Do we truly 'believe' in Him?

Those present in this Bible-study were listening with such intensity that they didn't want Jim to stop, and Jim himself was overcome with emotion when he stopped! They all sat back in their seats and wondered if, in fact, they had been visited by the Holy Spirit...who was present right there in their midst? Jim said, "I couldn't have said those words...I don't know that much about Jesus. The Holy Spirit just taught us a lesson and He used me to tell it." Amy looked at him and he was 'different' somehow. Even Summer noticed the change. Jim concluded by saying, "Well, I think we've finished this first session; let's pray. Thank you, Lord...for visiting us tonight. It was a lesson we will not soon forget. We give you all the praise and honor...glory to You in the highest! You are a great God! In Jesus name, Amen!"

Bill and May left first, then Jim started to leave. He kissed the kids goodnight and said how much he loved them. He put his arm around Amy and she walked him to the car. He didn't know why, but when they reached the car he went down on one knee and reached in his pants-pocket and pulled out a ring- box...opened it and looked up at Amy. He said, "From the first day I looked into your eyes, I was overcome with a love for you that will not go away! I've realized that I don't want to go home and say 'goodnight' anymore...I want to stay with you and the kids if you all will have me. Amy, I am so in love with you! Will you marry me?" Amy was so shocked! She was 'speechless' for a few moments...then said,

"Yes! Yes! Yes! I will marry you!" The kids were watching from the window and came running outside...threw their arms around Jim and all hugged each other in celebration of great happiness and well-being! "What a night!," said Amy.

13

THE WEDDING

An engaged woman with two children...but the world looks a lot different this morning! These were the thoughts of Amy Sky soon to be Amy Amico. Throwing the covers off, she smelled the coffee brewing. This was odd because she made the coffee every morning. Rushing down the stairs, she saw her 'man' making breakfast for the family. Jim said, "Don't hurry 'cause you have the morning off! Bill is filling in for you this morning."

Amy ran up to him and kissed him and said, "Good morning my love!" Summer and Jackson were sitting around the kitchen-island watching and loving every minute of the happiness that their mother and soon-to-be step-father were enjoying. Jim lived two houses down from Amy and making breakfast was no problem for him. He understood how people might talk about the possibility of his sleeping-over at night, but they don't know the man called 'Jim Amico.'

Summer blurted out, "Well! Are you two going to set a date for the wedding? As far as Jackson and I are concerned, the sooner-the-better!" Amy and Jim looked at each other and said, "I want the same thing," almost at the same time. Amy said, "Let's have a small wedding at our Church with Bill and May, how about it, Jim?" Jim replied immediately, "That sounds perfect to me! Are you sure you don't want something bigger? I know how some women feel about weddings." Amy insisted, "I just want to be your wife and the kids need a father-figure around our home." Jim said, "Alright then, I'll set it up...how about a week from this Saturday?" Amy lovingly agreed, "I like that."

Bill and May were wondering why Jim wanted Amy to have the morning off, when Jim arrived at the Coffee Shack with Amy, arm-in-arm. "Hi guys!" said Jim. "Amy and I have something to tell you!" May said excitedly, "Well, get on with it!" Jim didn't hesitate and said, "Last night I asked Amy to marry me and she said 'yes' and we want to get married a week from this coming Saturday! It's going to be a small wedding, just us and the kids and you two...if that's OK with you?" Bill replied, "I must say, you sure took your time!" Then he asked, "What made last night so 'crucial' that you popped-the-question?" Jim replied, "After being in the presence of God during our Bible study last night, I was overcome and it just came out! I purchased the ring a few days ago and I didn't know the right time to ask her. Last night just seemed right!"

Life took on new meaning for Jim and the Sky family...a wedding to prepare for, and for Jim, an experience so new it scared him! Imagine being alone all his adult life and now sharing everything with the one he loved so dearly! The Church was contacted and the pastor was pleased to hear the good news. He asked Jim and Amy to come to the Church so he could go over a few things. Jim agreed and set up Wednesday's appointment at 7:00 PM. The Coffee Shack now had a good working-crew; things were busy and nobody realized that Friday night and Saturday was when the Baseball finals were taking place! Jackson called out to Jim at the Coffee Shack and said, "What about the playoff finals?" Jim stopped, turned around and was speechless. Amy said, "The final game is taking place at 5:00 P.M., so there's no conflict with the wedding. We'll be done before that time and we'll be able to be at the game that night! Bill poked in and said, "You two are officially 'off' those two days! May and I will handle the Shack while you're getting ready for your wedding and that goes for the kids also."

Amy and Jim met with the pastor and went over the ceremony. Jim asked to take Communion and Amy wanted the candle ceremony, where one candle represented her and one candle represented Jim; then a large candle representing their marriage together, would be lit by taking the flames from the smaller candles. The Pastor agreed, so everything was set for 1:00 PM on Saturday. Pastor John asked Amy and Jim to be seated and said he wanted to take a little time to talk with them about married life. Pastor John began: "Amy, I'm sure you know much about the things that happen when two people get married; but I think Jim has 'no clue' of what is about to take place. You see, Jim...life will now be different and yes, exciting, but the things you did before will be changing. Let me give a 'for-instance;' you'll both share the same bathroom and that's my way of saying that your intimacy will not only be in your bedroom but it will be 'constant' during all of your days together. Everything will be done with your mate and your family in mind. Things you did without thinking will now take time to discuss with each other and your family. Jim, are you hearing what I'm trying to say?" Jim thoughtfully said, "I think so, Pastor. I'm not alone anymore and this is something new to me. I believe I'm understanding what you're saying. I've been thinking about this for several weeks and I've made up my mind that I'll be 'totally committed' to this marriage and this family. I know and I understand that this is a step that I cannot take lightly." Pastor John reiterated, "Great, Jim! I knew you were an intelligent man, but as a pastor, I needed to tell you that your lives will be changing. Jim and Amy thanked the Pastor for guidance. Hand-in-hand, Jim and Amy left the Church with renewed hope for a life full of love and a family that would bring them much joy.

Jim was really excited and he asked Jackson to be his best man. Jackson said, "That would be a real honor!" And Summer would be Amy's 'maid-of-honor,' so the whole family would be part of a day that they all would remember for the rest of their lives. After the meeting at the church, they had dinner at home...just the four of them.

At dinner, Summer said, "Jim, do you know when the trial starts?" Jim was startled by the question, but said, "No, I don't. But I'm sure it won't start until late August or early September. Why, is anything bothering you?" Summer said, "No, I just had a thought...that's all." Jim looked at her and said, "This trial will not be a big spectacle; it's an open and shut case, that's what I was told by the lawyers." Summer had reverted to thinking about what she'd experienced when she was kidnapped. Her heart began to race as the visions ran through her mind. She stopped and purposely turned her thoughts to her Lord and Savior; soon her heart recovered to its normal state. She wasn't scared, just concerned about the unknown. This wedding will bring joy and peace to their family and safety to her life.

It was the morning of the wedding and Amy awoke with a sense of happiness that she hadn't felt in an extremely long time. She recalled how 'alone' she felt when she lost her husband. Days were bearable because of her work and her family...but the nights never seemed to be extinguished. She had no one to tell of her deepest thoughts and troubles...no one to complete her wishes that were always there. Now her smile was like 'shining diamonds' that infected everyone around her. This morning, the kitchen was full of aromas that made her mouth water. Now some-one else was willing and able to help by making the waffles and frying the bacon-and-eggs. Amy could hardly wait to grab a fork and knife and be-gin to pour the hot maple syrup all over her waf-fles! The bacon was crisp with the eggs over-easy and everyone soon had their mouths full of joy. Jackson said, "If this is the kind of breakfast we're going to have every morning, I'll have to run a few more miles every day!" Everyone tried not to laugh because their mouths were so full! 'Clean-up' seemed to be much easier because they all pitched in to get the kitchen back to nor-mal.

Jim went back home after kissing all of his 'soon-to-be' family and began to get ready for the wedding. Jim told Jackson to come with him and he would help him get dressed. The women went to take their showers and get their hair ready. Summer did her mothers hair and Amy looked heavenly! Amy couldn't believe what a great job Summer had done! Amy had an easy job with Summer because she had naturally-wavy hair and once it was blown-dry, it looked like it took hours to complete. Amy helped her mother with her wedding dress...it was the same dress she wore at her first wedding. As the dress slid down over her body, she couldn't help but think of her first husband and tears filled her eyes. She missed him and she felt as if she were dishonoring him in some way by wearing this dress. Somehow, Summer 'knew' the emotions her mother was feeling. Amy recovered quickly, knowing that Jim was her future now...the past had to be left behind. She's once again experiencing true happiness because she's marrying the man that God sent to her when He heard her crying in those lonely nights after her husband Patrick died.

The day could not have been any better. The sun glimmered off of everyone's face as it did off the whole environment of the Church. The summer aromas brought a pleasantness that filled one's very being. The sense that something beautiful was taking place was all around. Jim and Jackson arrived at the Church first and were surprised at how many people were already in attendance. They entered the Church from a side-isle near the front and stopped at the altar. The Church began to fill up and Jim was getting very excited. The rings that he and Amy purchased were in Jackson's pocket. The organ began to play and Jim looked up and got his first glimpse of the woman that was about to be his bride. He was overwhelmed by what he saw! Amy was waiting in the back as her daughter walked down the center-isle and she followed. Brides have always had a glorious glow about them...especially on their faces! Jim was looking at her and the expression on his face was priceless. His smile reached from ear to ear and as she approached him, his eyes began to fill with tears. He loved this woman so much that it was hard to restrain himself. He took her hand and faced her and Pastor John began to read the words that would join them together. Soon came the time for them to say their vows to each other. Amy looked at his face and she was so intoxicated with the moment that it took awhile for her to say the words she had written down. She said, "Jim, you're the only man that I can now give my life to. The first time I saw you at the ball-field, I hoped you would be a part of our lives. As I started to get to know you better, I was stunned by the kind of man you are. The kindness that flowed from you and how tender you were with me and my children...that's when I fell in love with you. We became closer and with our very first kiss, I was convinced that I wanted you to be a major part of our lives. I will do my best to give you all the love you can contain. You are and will be...the world to me and my children. My excitement of being your wife is overwhelming! I love my God...our God...my children...our children...and you...with my entire being." Jim's face was wet with tears he couldn't hold back. She looked so gorgeous it was hard for him to concentrate on the words he wanted say. He took her hand, looked into her eyes and said, "Amy, you are the only woman I have ever loved. I couldn't have fallen in love with anyone better! Your love for your children and your love for our God...showed me the kind of woman you are. Amy, I love you with all of my being, and I will do everything in my power to protect and honor you and love you until the Lord takes me home. I promise to love your children as if they were my very own. I've asked God why I hadn't fallen in love with anybody before. For so many years, I've been lonely and haven't been all-that-happy with my life. So I came to Shadow and met the woman I have always dreamed about. The Lord answered my prayer; He's now shown me 'why' I've never before fallen in love. Today, He gives to me someone who is so beautiful, so understanding, so warm, and so wonderful to be around. I've asked Him many times if He's sure that I'm the one He wants to love this incredible woman that He's created! I believe that He created you for me...and I will do everything in my power to give you, Amy, Summer and Jackson...a life full of Love - Joy - Peace and Protection for as long as God will allow and enable me to give."

This new family then received Communion along with the rest of the Church. The candle-lighting was a magnificent ceremony as Jim and Amy took the flame from each of the candles that represented each of them and lit the candle that represented their unity. They kissed and walked down the isle and were stunned by the number of people that filled the Church. They were greeted in the Narthex of the Church by many well-wishers. Amy and Jim thanked them and Pastor John for making this such a glorious day to remember! When they reached the outside, they were showered with rice...some of which felt like 'darts,'so they got in the car 'fast' and the children followed. They went to Amy's house and looked at each other and kissed. The kids got out first and ran into the house and up to their rooms to change clothes and get dressed for the final base-ball-playoff-game. Amy and Jim went upstairs and entered what used to be Amy's room and held each other and kissed and kissed. She took off her dress and Jim undressed as they looked at each other. They wanted to..., but the kids were close by, so they restrained themselves. He looked at her and took her in his arms and said, "You are so beautiful and I'm so nervous!" Amy reassured him, "Don't be! We'll have a wonderful time together...you'll see." Jim told her that he'd

PB   Hawks

made a reservation in a nearby town for a brief 'honeymoon' and that Bill and May would take care of the kids for the next few days. "Is that OK with you?" he asked. Amy emphatically responded, "You mean I'm going to have you all-to-myself for at least a few days? Is that OK? You bet it is!" With her arms around him, she held him as close as time permitted.

They packed a few things and Jim said, "We'll leave right after the ball-game is over." So they made something to eat for themselves and the kids and went to the ball-game. When they got to the ball-field, everyone congratulated them and Bill told them, "You two can leave anytime you want!" They stayed until the fifth inning; Jackson's team was leading by ten runs and Jackson had already hit two home runs! So they looked at each other and went over to Jackson who said, "You guys don't have to stay...we've got this 'wrapped up!'"

Amy said, "OK, but be good and listen to Bill and May!" They went over to Summer...kissed her and she said, "What are two doing here? Go! We'll be fine!" So, the newlyweds were 'off-to-their-honeymoon!'

Amy was sitting close to Jim as they drove to the front of the Hotel. Jim took her by the hand and led her to the hotel desk. Their room was on the ocean- side and the view was beyond exquisite! The view was the last thing on their minds right then. They held each other and fell on... (words used at this time would devalue their wedding night...which should be between Amy and Jim only).

14

THE HONEYMOON IS OVER

After arriving home, Amy said, "I didn't tell you about an old high school friend that stopped by the Coffee Shack." Jim asked, "What made you think of that?" Amy responded, "I don't know exactly. It just popped into my head. I don't even know him very well; he hung out with a different group than mine." Jim asked, What's his name?" Amy said, "Ryan something...I can't remember his last name. Sounds like Caps or Naps ...something like that. He told me he wanted to come and help when he heard about Summer being kidnapped, but he had a terrible car crash and lost the ability to walk for a long period of time. He sounded like he had a crush on me...now as well as back in high school; maybe I'm reading too much into what he said." Jim pondered, Perhaps you re right, however it s something to keep in the back of our minds." Amy concluded by saying, "I hope I never see him again. He gives me the creeps!" Jim reached out for her and took her in his arms and said, "Let s not be concerned with that, it s you I want to think about!" Amy responded warmly, "Sure is good to be home, not that our honeymoon wasn't the greatest time I ever had!"

Jim and Amy made their way up the stone pathway to the door of the house and were surprised that no one greeted them. They opened the front door and found that the house was a mess! Very perplexed, Jim asked, "What happened here?" Just at that time, Summer, Jackson, May and Bill came running in. "Hi mom and dad!" said Summer and Jackson. "Hi-you-two! Are you alright? What happened here?" asked Amy. Summer anxiously said, "Two nights ago we went to the movies with Bill and May and when we returned home, the door was broken-into and whoever did it left this mess. So Bill took us to his house to stay until you returned." Bill said, "I called the police and they came immediately and advised us to stay somewhere else until you re-turned." We ll start cleaning up now," said Jack-son. "Hold on son! I wanna hear what you and Summer did while we were away," interjected Jim. Jackson said, "Did you hear me call you dad when you came home? I hope that s'OK' with ev-erybody." Jim responded, "Jackson, ever since I laid eyes on you, I always considered you as a young man. I m so proud that I m now in the fa-ther-role in this family! I'm overjoyed that you d call me   dad!'Summer joined in, "That goes for me too! OK dad?" Jim put his arms around the two of them and held them close. Amy came and joined in.

"Does anyone have any clues about who this intruder is?" asked Jim. "None so far," Bill said. "The police are going door-to-door around the neighborhood, asking if anyone had seen any-thing, but nothing s come up yet." Amy said, So now let s get this place cleaned-up and have some dinner! But first, let s make a list of any-thing that s missing. After a few hours of putting things in the right place and picking-up any bro-ken articles of glass, etc., the house looked good once again. After they had finished, no one had detected that anything was missing. May had din-ner ready; they sat around the table and Bill led evening- prayers. For the first time, they had dinner as a family with their good friends. Jackson and Summer picked-up the dishes and placed them in the dishwasher. After the dishwasher started, they gathered in the living room. "Why would anyone want to break into our home?" Jim asked. "I wonder if it has anything to do with the upcoming trial," said Summer. "I didn't even think about that," said Amy. "Jim, do you have all the clothes you need here?" Amy asked. Jackson exclaimed, "That s right! You live here now! We all sleep in the same house now! I wake up with my dad in the same house! Thank you, God!" Jim affirmed, .And that s the way it ll be until you begin a family of your own, which won't happen for few more years, so I hope this is something you both want." Jackson and Summer both came and put their arms around Jim and said, Besides mom, you re the best thing that s happened to this family...and we love having you as our dad! We know you can't take the place of our real dad, since he s in heaven, but we love having you step-in to fill his role! We love you Jim, and we want to call you dad, if that s OK with you!" Jim was visibly moved, and said, "I hope you know how much you guys mean to me! I may not be your real father, but I ll treat you as if I am. Calling me dad is a real honor to me!"

Evening came and after watching The Edge Of Tomorrow,   (the movie), they all decided to have prayer and go to bed. Summer-time was coming to an end and fall was in the night-air. Jim took a walk out on the back porch and a'chill came over him; he hadn't realized he need a jacket. He looked over the trees that jotted the landscape. How blessed he was, he thought, and just saying Thank You to the God Who put all this together didn't seem enough. God provided him with a love that he never-before experienced and a family that he loved so much...well, he was filled with gratitude and just had to express it with a big smile! Wow, what a night! Still he thought of the upcoming trial and how re-living all that mess again would not be pleasant for his new family, let alone the whole town.

Jim went back in the house, rubbed his arms to get warm and started to shut all the lights off when he smelled smoke. He immediately started looking around the house; he checked the kitchen, he checked the den, he checked the fire-place (the fire was out) and the heater was being used to take the chill out of the house. So he decided to check outside. He put a lite jacket on and opened the front door when Amy came down. She said, "Jim, where are you going?" "I smelled smoke and I couldn't find anything in the house that was burning, so I'm going to take a walk around the house for the source of that smell." She said, "I m sure it s nothing, but be careful! Here s a flashlight...and please shut the door." Jim took his time and looked closely around the house, but didn't find anything suspicious. He then noticed that two houses down the road, someone was burning some brush. He went down there to see what was happening. The brush was burning but there was no one around. This was against the city s laws; someone had to attend a fire at all times! Jim called-out for someone but no one answered. He got a bucket from Amy s house...took some water from a nearby stream and doused-out the fire. But this worried Jim. He looked around the neighborhood. Most of the homes were closing-down for the night and he didn't see anyone else on the streets. So he started for home. The house was dark except for a little light at the doorway. He got his bearings and started for Amy's room and soon had his pjs on and was in bed with his beautiful wife.

15

RYAN SHOWS HIS TRUE COLORS

Starting the day with a cup of coffee brought a smile to Jim s face...especially when he was the co-owner of the best Coffee Shack in town! Amy was so pleased with her family owned Coffee Shack! She opened the doors early around 5:30 AM to begin the adventure of a new day. Around 7:00am, the customers began filing in and things would start getting a little hectic. Amy loved greeting every one with a big smile and a "Good Morning!" She never realized how beautiful she was and what a presence she made behind the counter.

Everything was going like every other day until Ryan showed-up and ordered a Latte. "I read you got married." Amy answered, "Yes," then wondered what he was doing there. "Well, I was hoping you d go to lunch with me". Directly to the point, since she was already busy, she said: "What do you want, Ryan?" He responded, "Just want to be friendly." Amy snapped back, I don't think going to lunch with you is a very good idea." Ryan recoiled, "I see! You re just the same as you were in high school! You were always too good to go out with a man like me! You hung-out with your friends and never noticed someone like me. Someone who would have done anything for you, but no, you just ignored me!" Amy stopped him and said, "I think you should leave". He looked back as he started for the door and said, "Amy, you ll be sorry for this...you ve already had a taste of some of the grief for the way you treated me years ago," as he closed the door behind him. Amy was visibly upset and she couldn't figure out what had just happened. She took her cell-phone and called Jim. He answered her call but before he could say hello, she broke out with, "Jim! Do you have time to come over to the Shack? I need to talk with you about that guy

Ryan I told you about." Jim responded, "OK, I ll be right over!" Jim's arrival was greeted with Amy's arms wrapping around his neck as he said, "What s the matter, sweetheart?" She told him that Ryan was there just a few minutes ago and said some things that really shook her up! "He asked me to go to lunch with him,"she said.   I told him that it wouldn't be a good idea. He said that I ignored him in high school and that I would be sorry for that and that I ve already tasted some of the anguish for how I treated him! What did he mean by that?" Jim remained calm, but said, "I don't know, but could it be he was involved with what happened to Summer?" Amy cried out, "Oh my God! Could that be true?" Jim went out on the deck and called Bill, saying, "I think we have a lead on what happened to Summer. I think we ve got a guy who may be involved!" Jim relayed what happened at the Coffee Shack between Amy and Ryan. "Who is this .Ryan'guy?" Bill asked. Jim responded, "He s someone who went to high school with Amy." Bill quickly surmised, "OK, she went to Shadow High School so it won't be hard to find him and track him down. Should I call the police?" Jim said, "No, not yet. I want to get more information about him before we call anyone about this. Perhaps I can get to talk to him." Bill asked if Jim knew his last name. "I don't know exactly, but Amy said it sounds like Haps or Caps.'Bill exclaimed, "Could it be Knaps?'Jim said, "Maybe that s it!" Bill replied, "Then he might be the son of Sid Knaps, the guy we caught and soon will be on trial!" Jim said in an elevated and somewhat angry tone: "Wow! Bill, will you check him out from the time he went to high school until today?" Bill volunteered, "Sure! I can do that!" Jim said, "Good! I m going to check around town. Perhaps I can get to talk to him. Once we do this preliminary investigation, maybe we ll be able to notify the police about what happened!" Bill agreed, "OK! I'll get on it right now!"

Amy closed the coffee shack after a long day and drove home. She started to think about her high school years. She thought back and tried to remember how Ryan was back then. She remembered how much he annoyed her by trying to be part of the group she was hanging around. When she first saw him, she only remembered saying no to him when he asked her to go to the prom with him. However, now she began to remember how much he tried to be part of her life. She kept pushing him away and she guessed he got the impression that she didn't think he was worthy of being around her and her friends. So now he has a vendetta against her and her family. Jim

thought to himself that if Ryan s somehow involved with what Summer had to go through, he
d make sure he suffered dearly...one way or another. Amy was approaching her house when, as
Amy told Jim, she thought she saw someone out
of the corner of her eye, but when she focused in
that direction, no one was there. Maybe she was
so upset, that she thought she was just seeing
things.'Even when she reached her door, she
couldn't help looking over her shoulder.

Summer was making dinner with May; Jim and
Bill were in the den and Jackson was glued to the
T.V. "Hi mom!" said Summer. Jackson repeated his
sister s greeting and Jim came out, kissed her
and said, "How was your day, sweetheart?"
Somewhat nervously, she said, "Edgy...after what
happened, but good after you left; that is, until I
started to approach the house. I thought I saw
someone out of the corner of my eye, but I guess
it was just my nerves." Jim reassured her, "Bill
and I are checking this guy Ryan's background. I
m sure we'll find out if anything's going on. He
does have the same last name as the man we
caught in what happened to Summer." Amy
blurted out, "What? Are you kidding me?" Jim
calmly said, "No, his last name is the same, we
just don't know if they re related as yet." Amy exclaimed, "OH! I think they are! I thought it was

just when he asked me to the prom, but I remember more. He always wanted to get into the same group I was in. I did everything to push him away, so now he s trying to get back at me by hurting my family!" Just then, Bill received a call...then reported to Jim:"I just heard from a friend who s on the force; he checked out Ryan Knaps for me. He s a bad guy! He and his father were arrested for drugs and graft. They did five years and were released about a year ago. He said to tell you to protect yourself because these two are dangerous! He said it s not a good idea to approach them in any way and to please allow the police to do their jobs! Jim vigorously said, So they are connected! Bill replied, As connected as you can get...father and son!" Jim postulated, "Perhaps they were both involved in capturing Summer and the father violated her! So they both were in on it! So what must we do now?" Jim announced that they needed to get the family together and talk about what should be done!

Jim called all the family together including Bill and May. "Look! We re dealing with some bad creeps, so we must be smart and never approach them in any way. Should Ryan come into the Coffee Shack again, call me and the police. Summer! It s important that you and Jackson never go anywhere alone! If you can't stay together, make sure you re always with someone, never alone! Do you understand?" They shook their heads in agreement. Jim continued, "That goes for us adults too! We could be in danger, so we must pay attention and be cautious about everything we do. I m not trying to startle you, but if we re not vigilant, we could find ourselves in a bad situation! We also don't know if there are more than these two involved. So from now until the trial, we must be as careful and as observant as we can be! It might mean our very lives.

Ryan was staying in small cabin in the near-by woods. The cabin was not far from Jim and Amy's house. He had been planning to get his father out of jail. He knew he might have to ask someone to help, but he didn't have anyone in town to help him. He decided to get someone from California and he knew just who he would choose. First, he had more ideas about how to deal with Amy and her family; they hadn't seen the last of him! He wanted to make sure she never forget throwing him aside in high school! His dad had done his job when he kidnapped Summer. As he understood it, his dad had done a complete job on her before her step-dad broke-in on him. Ryan swore that he do his best to make the step-dad regret his part in that action! Ryan's hate for Amy had overwhelmed him for years. As thoughts filled his mind about his next steps, he began to wonder why this Amy-person had dominated his life so much? Was it because of her beauty or her shape? He didn't really know, but it burned inside him and he had to satisfy his hate with action even if it meant his death...the death of Amy...or even Amy's family.

16

RYAN BEGINS HIS TERROR

The family got ready for bed and Bill and May were heading home   when Jim called out and said, "Before you go and before the kids go to bed lets pray." Bill and May stopped at the door and came back to the living room and they all knelt to pray. "Father, we come in the name of Jesus. We find ourselves in a pretty bad situation. Two men have come to town for the purpose of harming our family. I pray for your protection and your strength. Allow the Holy Spirit to show us what to do and to enlighten the police on how to handle these men without harm coming to anyone in our family and that also means Bill and May, We thank you Father for Your love and we trust that You will bring this to the best conclusion possible. In Jesus name we ask."

The kids found their way to bed and sleep and Amy is getting ready for bed. Jim is sitting up in bed thinking of the day's events, considering how best to protect his family. Relying on the local police didn't seem the most secure strategy. Nevertheless, what else did he, have available to secure his family's well being. Perhaps hiring a private detective to shadow Summer and Jackson, but what about Amy, Bill and May? Can't afford that many private detectives. The more he thought about it the more he just couldn't figure it out. Just as Amy moved into bed Jim decided to get up and take a walk to see if he could come to some conclusion. "I'll be back in a few minutes I just have to take a walk to clear my head."

The night was a little chilly but clear. The stars shone brightly with a moon as big as a glow ball. Jim walked outside slowly around the house to check for anything out the ordinary. He found nothing so he directed his sights to the surrounding neighborhood. That's when he saw something moving in a nest of trees directly across the street. He stayed hidden and observed the movement, was it an animal or human? He saw a pair of eyes shining in the moonlight, but still didn't know if it was human or not. He stayed calm as

the movement came into the street. He was anxious when he noticed the figure was of a man
could this be Ryan Naps. What is he doing this
time out at night in his neighborhood. He must be
up to no good, he thought, but when he just
started walking down the street away from Jim
and Amy's house Jim believed he just out for a
walk. He didn't think Ryan saw him, so what was
this all about, he wondered. Jim found his way
back to bed and Amy was in a heavy sleep as Jim
pulled the covers up to his chest and settled in.
Sleep took over and the house was quiet for the
night.

Ryan took a short walk down the street until
he broke into a run across to neighbor's back yard
and made his way to the main objective. When
Jim and Amy's house was in sight he clinged tight
to the back yard wall of their house he made his
way to just outside of the den window and knelt
down. He took out a wad of newspaper and piled
some trigs on the paper that he had gathered
from the surrounding area. Soon the match was
struck and a fire developed that he hoped would
begin to ignite the house on fire. He ran across
the street and hide in the adjacent woods. He observed what he started until he was sure the
house was burning and then he made his way

back to the cabin. Ryan didn't know that he was spotted by Jim just before the fire started.

Smoke filled the house and the alarms began to sound off. Jim awoke as did Amy and they started to wake the kids and yelled get out don't take anything with you... just get out of the house. As soon as Jim saw Amy and the kids were out ,the fire trucks pulled up to the front of the building. However Amy had to get something and ran back into the fire filled house. Jim yelled don't Amy but she was in the front door before he could stop her. Jim was panicking and told a fireman about Amy he said, "Stay here we will get her out." They returned with Amy but she was unconscious and the fire burned her back and right arm. Firemen did their work fast and efficiently but as hard as they tried the house was lost completely. That wasn't as important as the condition of Amy, she was loaded into the ambulance headed to Shadow General Hospital. The emergency room was almost empty, so she was taken care of at once. She was still unconscious oxygen was given and her face was cleaned removing the smoke stains. Jim was in the waiting area when Bill and May came in, he conveyed to them what had happened. "Why did she run back into the house," Bill insisted. Jim was so worried about Amy didn't think about Summer and Jackson when he mentioned them to May, she said that they were taken to their house clearing their throats of smoke. They want to come here to be their mom. When Jim looked up they were standing in front of him, they said that the fireman brought them here. Jim embraced them and told them how much he loved them "Your mom is going to be al lright, I just know it" They held each other close and sat down. Soon after they arrived to the hospital, the doctor came up to Jim. "How is she doctor" "She still a little groggy and the burns on her right side are only second degree. However, I am not saying that they are minor, they have to be treated with care, but they will produce little scaring if treated properly." "Thank you, when can we see her, give the nurses a little time and they will notify you when you can go in.

Everything was lost, furniture, pictures, computers, everything. The only good thing was Jim's house was just a little ways down the street. So having a place to sleep was not going to be a problem. Bill and May insisted they stay at their house. Bill said, "You are staying at our place tonight." "It's OK, Bill my home is not far." "I don't care you are all coming to my house until we can figure out what happened, and I am not taking no. Is that understood." "OK, but I'm staying here with Amy. Summer and Jackson said, "Do we have to go dad," they asked." "Listen go to May's and get cleaned up and drink plenty of water, rest and I'll see you in a few hours and we will go shopping for clothes and other things we need."

Ryan seeing the house go up in flames put a smile on his face. Until, when turning on his TV. in his cabin, and hearing that Amy was injured, he didn't want that to happen. He couldn't hold back his tears, his love for Amy overwhelmed him. He wanted that guy Jim to get hurt and not his beautiful Amy. He tried to call the hospital to find out her condition, but the hospital would not give out any information because of the ongoing investigation."What investigation" "The fire was started by an individual, it was not an accident." "Oh! I see" Ryan said and hung up the phone. He thought, nobody saw me that night so nothing will lead them to me.

Jim was sitting on a chair adjacent to Amy's bed when he looked up, he saw two strangers approaching Amy's room. They came up to the doorway and asked if they could speak to Jim. Jim went into the hall and said "What can I do for you" they pulled out their badges and said, "We are investigating your house fire. I see the owner is Amy Sky is that correct." "Yes, that's correct, we were married a few weeks ago" You are the same person who contacted us about a break in, is that correct." "Right again, but nobody showed up from the police." "Well, we are here now. Let's start with what is your name." "I am Jim Amico" "So tell me what you know about this fire." I was so shaken about the break in I couldn't sleep so I took a walk around the house to see if everything looked ordinary, all was good until I noticed something moving in the woods across the street. I stayed hidden and I watched, it was Ryan Naps walking out of the woods and down the street. When I saw him walking away from the house I felt everything was OK." "Well the neighbors did see you walking around the property of Mrs. Sky." "You mean Mrs. Amico" "Yes of course, did you start the fire Mr. Amico." "No, I didn't and what kind of question is that, are you thinking I had anything to do with burning down of my wife's house. You got to be kidding me." " We have an obligation to follow up on every lead. You were spotted walking around the house minutes before it went up in a blaze." " Maybe you are not famil-iar with the Naps family. The father, Sid Naps kid-napped my step-daughter a few months ago and will be going on trial in October." "No, we didn't know that. We will have a talk to him." "Tell him that I saw him last night and he will not get away with this." "As long as you don't take the law into your own hands." "If you do your jobs officers, I won't have to." " Thank you for the information we'll see you soon.

Jim turned around and returned to Amy's bedside. Holding her hand, he thought how wonderful it has been since coming to Shadow, thank God Amy is going to be alright after she recovers from this act of terror on our family. Amy's arm bandage had to be changed so Jim was going to leave while the nurses changed her bandage "No I want you to stay and see how this is done, because if she is to return home you or someone will have to do this each day," said the attending nurse. Jim observed the process intently. When it was over, the nurse indicated that when she leaves, there will be a sufficient amount of bandages to take home with them.

Jim knelt down and prayed "Lord what a nightmare we just went through. I ask that You protect our family from all evil and heal my wife Amy from the burns she suffered and heal us all from this terror. In Jesus name, Amen" Just when he finished his prayer Amy opened her eyes and looked at Jim. She said, "I am sorry Jim" "What made you go back in that burning building." "I had to get my wedding rings. They mean so much to me, you mean so much to me, I couldn't let this evil man take that away from me" she emphasized. "Sweetheart, we can always get another ring, but we can't get another you." "I know I didn't think it would take that long, I'm sorry." "Thats over now let's consecrate, on your healing and recovery. How are you feeling?" "I'm doing fine the pain is not bad, how do I get out of here." "It might be tomorrow the doctor said so take time to rest I'll be here" "OK my love" she said, and closed her eyes

Jim's thoughts turned to Ryan and what kind of lies he is telling the police as Amy falls off to sleep. He was determined to stop this man from doing any more harm to his family. He would get together with Bill when Amy is finely home. Perhaps he knows some retired cops that could help with a course of action to take. Jim leaned back in his chair and drifted off to sleep. Dreams can take you to places you have no idea of where or how they lead you. Jim was having that kind of dream. He was lost somewhere and he was looking for a bad man. A man that took the life of a child because he observed a drug deal and he took the boy out (killed him) so there would be no witnesses.

17

FAMILY IN THEIR NEW HOUSE

Ryan wanted to get more information about Amy, so he took a chance and went to the hospital. He tried checking with the nurse on her floor, but didn't get any news about Amy because he was not a member of the family. So he decided to go home but was stopped by two men. "Aren't you Ryan Naps?" They asked.

"Yes, what do you want?" "What are you doing here?" Asked the two men. Ryan was a little lost for words. "I was... checking on my neighbor her house was burned tonight." "You are not a relative are you?" "No, I'm not," said Ryan. "Couldn't you wait until tomorrow and ask a member of the family?" "Sure, that would be best, I'll do that, " Ryan agreed. "Well, now that we got you here, we would like to ask you a few question?"

"All right," Ryan said timidly. "Where were you tonight?" I was watching TV, "You were seen on the street where Amy Amico's house was burned." " I was." "Yes, you were," said the two men. "Who are you guys?" Ryan asked. "We are detectives from the Shadow Police Department," the men explained. "I'm telling you I was home all night until I came here to find more information about Mrs. Amico." "What were you watching on your TV?" "Nothing much just something on the History channel," said Ryan. "That's not really an answer Mr. Naps, could you tell us a little more?" The detectives asked. "Something about the early settlers from England," said Ryan. "How long was this show you were watching?" " I don't know it started at around 4:00 pm until I fell asleep. I was startled by something on the TV and when I got up I saw a house on fire even more so when I notice that the house was Mrs. Amico," Ryan explained."

"Ok you can go but don't leave town for any reason unless you check with the Police Department." Ryan returned home and was more than a little upset. First he knew that it was wrong going to the hospital. Then who could have seen me tonight on Amy's street? I bet it was that husband of hers. I'll have to do something to that guy that he'll remember for a long time, he was thinking.

Summer was with Bill and May and she was upset about the fire and her mom. Even though everyone sees her as healed from the circumstances of being kidnaped and raped, she is far from being healed. She still has nightmares and can't stop thinking about how ashamed she feels. The sick feeling she gets when those thoughts pop-up, nobody sees these things when they happen and she has not confided in anyone as yet. She is slowly losing it and doesn't know what to do. She wanted to talk with her mother, but after what she is going through it doesn't seem fair to put this on her too. So she decides to speak to Jim. Since becoming her step-dad, he is the strong one in the family, he's the one that found her and he would not give up until he did. He is the only one who would understand and the only real hope she has right now.

Amy was getting ready to go home, cleaning up putting things away. Even one night in the hospital is too much. She wanted to go home to relax and put all this behind her than she realized she has no home, she will be going to her husband's home. Amy has never felt so secure and loved by anyone before, her first husband loved her, but he was never home much because of being overseas and fighting a war. Jim was different his first concern is always about the family which made her feel calm and in peace. She thought she knew what love was all about being married before and in love with Jesus, but this time is different. She didn't know if it was because of Jim or because she is older now and can appreciate what love is all about. So this will be a new beginning for her, being in a different house, with a man she loves so dearly. She is proud of her children, being raised by a single parent they know so much about life and God to carry with them. They took to Jim so gracefully and made him feel like a true father. Putting her arm in Jim's arm they went out the door of the hospital. She truly was happy except for the fire and burns on her back and arm, she wanted to forget what happened go home as if nothing took place. That was not going to happen because this monster named Ryan was haunting her family.

Jim had called the kids to meet them at Jim's house. When he pulled up the driveway the kids greeted their mom with hugs and kisses. She was home and a little tired, so Jim took her upstairs and she laid on the bed and was out as soon as her head it the pillow. Jim covered her up and went downstairs to talk to the kids. "Hey, would you like to take a tour of your new house?" "Yes, I want to see it all," said Summer.

So they were shown the first floor, which consisted of the kitchen, the living room, the den toilet and washroom and a guest bedroom and toilet. The back yard was open with no fences the house was on a two acres piece of land. The second consisted of three bedrooms, the master and Summer's and Jackson's rooms, each with their own toilets. After that, Jackson was interested in fixing up his room, can you imagine that? Summer and Jim were alone in the den, when she looked at him and said "we have to talk." "Sure, sweetheart what's on your mind."

It's about what happened. You know when he took me and well...you know." "Yes, I do know." "Dad-Jim I can't talk to mom not after what she has gone through, I'm talking to you because I don't know who else to talk too." She said as tears started to run down her face. Jim took her in his arms and said, "things, are going to be all right." She said, "I'm going crazy, I can't sleep because I have these nightmares, sometimes when I'm walking home from school, I have flash-backs and I see him doing," she paused and cried harder. "I don't know what to do, I try to put on a good front but I can't control it anymore." "Sweetheart, it's understandable after what you went through," Jim said with his heart breaking. " I'm not a female so I don't understand fully what you went through, but I will try to help as much I can. " Dad, I feel like I'm dirty because what he did, I feel unclean every time I walk by someone. I feel like I want to die." She said as she buried her head in his chest. He took her by her shoul-der looked in the eye and said, "You are the most wonderful child a man could ask for and on top of that you are a child of the living God. That means you are loved, when you asked Jesus into your life you became a new creature, meaning your spirit is as perfect as it will ever be no matter what someone does to you. You still belong to Him. You said yourself that He was holding you in His arms. He's not holding this against you be-cause he is so in love with you just like me and your mother. My sweet girl don't take this burden on yourself. There was nothing you could have done to prevent this from happening. It was our evil enemy that did this. You are and always will be your Father's girl and nothing can take you out His hand, nothing. You are clean and beautiful and when you find a man to marry, he will see you the way your heavenly Father see you. Did you hear what I said." "Yes dad I did and but" He stopped her and said, "No but's, don't allow thoughts to come into your mind and distort what really happened. You must fight any thoughts that tell you...you, are at fault, because you are not. " OK dad, I can't tell you how much better that makes me feel. I promise that when I'm feeling down I will come to you and only you. I love you so much dad," she said as Jim held her tight. "I know that this is not going to go away fast It will bother you now and then, but you can always come to me and don't have to say a word I'll know what's happening" thanks dad.

Jackson, Summer and Jim all took part in making dinner. Jim went up to Amy and woke her up and asked her about dinner she indicated she wanted to eat with the family. So Jim and Amy went downstairs and sat at the table. They held hands and prayed, "Father we are deeply grateful for the protection You have given to us and ask that you bless us and this food we are about eat. Heal Amy quickly from the burns that she sustained from the fire. We ask all this in the name of Jesus Christ."

"This is our first meal in our new house, " said Amy."

18

RYAN MAKES PLANS

The morning brought low clouds that linger low in the branches of the tall trees. Jim kissed Amy and started the process of changing her bandages as he was shown in the hospital. First, he had to remove the old bandages which at times caused a great deal of pain to Amy. Slowly he pulled the bandages from her burns trying not to hurt her more than ordinary, sometimes he was successful and sometimes the gaze struck to her burn scars, which was unavoidable, but the pain she feel struck Jim's heart. After fifteen min‐ utes the process was finished and Amy was sit‐ ting up in bed with new bandages on and ready for the new day. Jim left her with a big kiss and gave her strict instructions to rest and not do too much in her new home. Jim was going over to the Coffee Shack to start the day. When he got there, Bill had already opened and was in full swing selling coffee to the town folks and, of course, everyone started asking about how Amy was doing. He thought this would be a daily inquisition, so he better get her well quickly.

Jim asked Bill if he came across any of his police friends that could help with the protection of his family. Bill indicated that three of his buddies will be by at 2:00pm today. "Great," Jim said, "We will meet on the deck." Jim called Amy every hour to see how everything was going. He worried every time they were out of his sight. He wanted to bring this to an end soon. This Nap family has hurt his love ones enough and it is time to end this thing now.

At 2:00 o'clock, the men were introduced to Jim "Hi, I'm Jack Stanley, hi, I'm Bo Hardly, hi, I'm Mike Jonas" "Glad to me you," Jim said.

Jack spoke first, "We were told about what you and your family have been through lately and we want to help." "Great what is the plan," Jim wanted to know.

"Bo is from California and knows someone who told him that Ryan was asking around for someone to help him in the Oregon area. We thought Bo would volunteer to help, this way we will know their plans and how we could stop him. Mike and I will keep your family in our sight for protection." "How is Bo going to make contact with Ryan?" asked Jim. Leave that up to us, this is not our first rodeo, so to speak." Jack pointed out. "OK, will you keep me up to date as to what is going on," Jim asked. "Yes, we will come into town asking for jobs. One of them should be right here in the Coffee Shack and Mike will work for Bill across the street in his shop," said Jack. "How much will this cost?" Asked Jim. Let's get the work done first, and then we talk about compensation later," said Jack.

Bo contacted his friend in California and asked how to contact this guy Ryan. The man said he lives in a small cabin outside of the town of Shadow and gave Bo Ryan's phone number. "Great thanks, hey can you call him so he knows that I will be coming." "Sure, I could do that" Bo was confident that he could make contact with Ryan without him being suspicious of anything.

"Ryan, this is Spike from California" "Hey, what do you want." "You asked me about a guy you can use up there, well I found you a guy his name is Bo and I gave him your number, he should be calling you in the next day or so." "Ok

Spike, this guy better be good." "He knows the area he used to live around there." "Great, I can't wait to meet him I have a lot of work for him to do." Ryan ended the call and wondered how much he could trust him at the beginning or should he just let him work and see how he does.

Jackson was playing football with his friends at the park and Summer was home reading outside on the back deck. It was late summer and the beginning of school was up fast. Her mind was on something other than school. The trial starts in October just a month and a half away. Butterflies started in her stomach and she began to get sick. I can't face that man again after what he did to me she thought. She stopped thinking about the future and began to pay attention to the book once again. It was a love story that takes place in the mountains of Colorado in the early 1930's, when she heard Jim coming up the drive. She knew it was him by the sound his truck made. She ran to the front door and welcomed him home, he was startled and she said "I'm scared dad"

"What's the matter?" "I was just thinking about how close the trial is and I just got off track little." "That's ok, we got to watch what we think about all the time, that's where the enemy gets to us." " I'm just glad your home, I feel much better when you are here." "How is your mom doing?" "She is out in the back working on her garden," "I told her to take it easy," " leave her dad, she's been in the house for three days she needed to get out for a while. She is doing good since she came home." "I have to change her bandages and put some clean dressing on."

She will be in shortly, I made some fresh coffee, I'll get you a cup."

"So what have you been doing?" "Just reading getting ready for school, which will be starting soon." "Where is Jackson?" "He is playing with his friends at the park" "I told you both not to go anywhere alone. I got to go and check on him, tell mom, I'll be home with Jackson soon."

Jim took the car to the park and looked for Jackson, but could not find him. He started asking everyone about him and one said he went to get a drink at local 7 Eleven. So he headed for the store and just about to enter when Jackson came out. "Hey son I have been looking for you."

"Dad we were just playing some football" "Good, is everything OK," "Yes, Oh I forgot we were not supposed to go anywhere without someone with us I'm sorry dad." "Come get in the car and I'll take you home," Jackson hopped in the car. "Look Jackson nothing happened this time but you don't know if it will be 'OK' the next

time so please don't do this again." "I won't."
"Look Jackson I hired some men to keep an eye
on us as a family but we must follow the rules I
set out for us or something could happen to one
of us and all of us will get hurt deeply. Jackson I
don't want to stop you from playing with your
friends or going places, but right now we need to
be careful." "I understand dad, thanks."

Bo called Ryan for the first time they set a
place and time to meet that day. It was 5:00 pm
and walking up to the cabin Ryan told him about.
At the door stood a man in his middle fifty and he
could tell he was carrying a gun under his jacket.
"You must be Ryan," Bo said. "Bo is that you."
Yes, it is said Bo, how are you?" " Ok, come in
and let's get down to business. First of all, do you
know anything about explosives?" Bo nodded his
head, "Yeah, a little." "Where do you get this
knowledge?" "On the Third Street Reds" a gang I
belonged to north of San Francisco." " What did
you do with them? "We blow up a school building
to rob money from the school office during the
summer of 2008." "Great you just the man I
need." "What do you have in mind," Bo asked?
"We are going to blow up a court house and free
my father who is going on trial for rapping some
kid that I told about."

Bo knew this guy was up to no good, but blowing up a court house that was a little over the top. He called a meeting and got together with Jack and Mike and told them about Ryan's plan. "This is bigger than we anticipated, we should bring the police in on this," said Jack. "No", said Bill as he came in the room, I know someone in the FBI, I'll ask him what to do. "I watched as you guys came into the building and I figured something was up, so I apologize for breaking in. We can't let this get out to anybody, not a sole, do you understand." "Ok, Bo you keep going along with the plan and let's meet here tomorrow night at this time." "Make it one hour later."

19

RYAN STEALS DYNAMITE

Jim closed the Coffee Shack for the day, he looked at his watch it was 7:10 PM. I have to get home and have dinner, he thought. Ryan watched as he closed the building for the night. Ryan knew that getting to Jim around this time of the day would be easy. Not tonight, he thought. He walked the other side of the street, keeping in the shadows, until Jim got in his car. Ryan went home for the night and a meeting with Bo.

Jim was pleased to see the family preparing dinner and Bill and May were present also. The dinner was great as always and the men cleaned the dishes and the kitchen and went into the living room. "I think Ryan is coming after you, Jim," said Bill. "What makes you say that Bill" "the way he looked at you when I seen him last."

"When did you see him last" " I didn't tell you, I went back to the hospital the night of the fire, and saw Ryan with two men. They looked like detectives and they were asking him questions. When they said that he was seen that night walking down the street. He knew the only one that could have seen him was you."

"That's right, " claimed Jim. "So he will be coming after me soon, that is great". May said, "Why is that great." "Knowing that I'm the one he is coming after, we can set up something to catch him." I'll tell Jack, Mike and Bo and my FBI friend," said Bill. Somebody better tell Shadow Police what is going on," said May. Bill said he would take care of telling the police and the FBI.

Ryan turned the TV off when he heard the knock on the door. It was Bo. "You're late, " said Ryan. "I know, but when I tell you why you'll understand." Bo leaned over and said in a quiet voice "I know where to get some explosives." Ryan's eye bows went up and excitement in is voice. "Where is this stuff," Ryan asked with ea-gerness. There is logging camp up Shadow Moun-tain, it's pretty far up. Well, I heard they brought in a supply of dynamite just a day or so ago." Ryan said, "That's stuff is very volatile, you got to take care when transporting it." "We will" What do you mean, we," Ryan said. "Look Ryan this must done at night and it will take two people to pull it off and that's you and me. Unless you have someone else that's working for you that I don't know about," Bo stated. "No, it's just you and me," said Ryan "When do we go and get this done. "Tomorrow night at midnight, dress warm and wear gloves and boots. I'll come by at 10:00 pm I'm going to rent a jeep and have padded box for the dynamite.

Bo went to the meeting that night with his army buddies. When he entered the room, Jack, Mike and Bill were already there. Bo told them about stealing the dynamite tomorrow night at the logging camp. "We could get him at the log-ging camp, "said Jack. "No, because we have nothing on him about the fire at Jim's house and the plan for breaking out of his father, he'll get away with only a small amount of time," Bill stated. "We will let him steal the dynamite and add it to the list of things we can put on him later." Jack said, "OK, that's a plan." "But Bill you must let the authorities know what's going on especially about stealing dynamite." "I can do that," said Bill.

Shadow mountain received the night's darkness with a quiet mist of rain. The mist made it uncomfortable to move around and be still. Bo after picking up Ryan at 10:00 drove the forty or so miles to reach the outskirts of the logging camp. It was midnight by the time they arrived and a chill was filling the air. This was all to formula to Bo and so unreal for Ryan, having never before been in a situation like this, but he followed Bo's lead. When the gate that surrounded the camp was reached Bo took the large wire cutters and made an opening in the fence. Growling through they found themselves behind a large tent. No guards were seen, and why should there be this was just a logging camp, no one expected someone would steal their dynamite. Bo cut a hole in the tent and reached in and took four sticks of dynamite, looked at Ryan and said "Do we need more than four sticks" " I think we more like six or eight" Bo added two more sticks and started to crawl through the hole in the fence when he heard a voice say "Did you hear anything out there Joe" "No I didn't hear anything Bobby go back to sleep" "Ok Joe"

That was the first indication of any guards in

the camp, Bo put his finger to his lips to indicate to Ryan to be quiet. Ryan nodded and followed Bo through the hole they didn't say anything until they reached the jeep. Bo placed the dynamite in the special box he made and closed the cover on the box they closed the jeep's door gingerly and didn't start the engine. Bo released the brake and rolled the jeep down the hill until they were far enough away from camp. The jeep started and they were on their way home without anyone noticing. Ryan looked at Bo, "So you've done this kind of thing before"

"A few times," Bo indicated. "Had no idea you were so experienced" "I was part of a gang that did these kind of things often, I thought I told you that before," Bo pointed out. "Yea, yea your right I lost my thinking a little," Ryan blatted out.

There wasn't much of a conversation in the jeep going back to Ryan's place. Bo pulled into the drive and took the box from the jeep and placed it in Ryan garage. Ryan said, "I don't want that stuff here." "Well do you have a better place for it" "No, can't you take it and put it somewhere safe." "Look you told me more than once that you run this show, if you wanted this stuff somewhere else You should have made some arrangements." "OK leave it here, but put it in a safe place away from everyone's eyes." "When is the trial anyway,"

Bo asked. "Two weeks from Tuesday and I need you here tomorrow to go over the plans and coordinate everything, I want this to go like a well oiled machine." "I'll be here tomorrow at noon." Bo said going through the door to his jeep.

20

WHAT A DAY

"What a day!" yelled Summer. This morning was truly awesome with the sun shinning and no clouds in the sky! The wind was one of the ele-ments that gave a glimpse of the fall season fill-ing the air. Fall brings the start of the rainy sea-son throughout most of Oregon. That means a whole new way of life in the northwest, when rain is part of the daily routine and indoor activities take over.

Amy was excited! She was back at her job at the Coffee Shack! Once again she started early in the morning with her preparations and she was looking forward to welcoming the towns-folk. She realized that this opening would be the first since her house had been burned-down. She was feeling good; the burns on her arm and back, although not totally healed, were feeling good-enough not to hinder her work. The folks started filing-in for their morning coffee and of course, most of them were asking how she was doing in her recuperation process. She felt alive again and that made her feel even better!. Her aware-ness of her surroundings was drilled into her by Jim and Bill, so she looked around the area a lot, especially during those first days back. Also, hav-ing Jack in the store helped a great deal, knowing he, had-her-back, which was a tremendous relief for her!

School started for Summer and Jackson who were taken to school by Mike. He wouldn't walk with them, he let them take the school-bus but tagged along in his car until he watched them en-ter school. He spent the rest of the day at Bill's shop (Bill is also the Postmaster for the town of Shadow and is busy with mailing and receiving packages of all kinds during the day). The kids were instructed to stay together except when in class. Mike would make sure they got on the school bus, followed the bus home and of course, waited for them to enter their house. He would wait a few more hours until an adult from the family arrived home.

This was the pattern...the way-of-life for Jim and his family until the trial started. Jim spent most of his day seeking out information about Ryan and his father. He was walking up the street where his family now lives when he noticed something odd in the woods across from their house. So he went to investigate and found a sight or scope which was like something one would put on a rifle or a gun. Who would have dropped something like this?   he thought.   It must be Ryan, checking us out at night. This has got to stop! He called Bo and when he answered, Jim said, "Can you talk?" Bo said, "Sure Jim. I'm home...what's up?" Jim continued, I'm across the street from my house and I found a scope lying on the ground. I think Ryan is watching us at night. Maybe his finger-prints are on it. I m going to give it to Bill so he can have his FBI friends check-it-out. But for now, can you stop him?" Bo reassured him, "Sure Jim. I'll make sure he keeps away from your house." Jim responded, "Thanks Bo. Is there anything that I should be aware of?" Bo concluded the conversation by saying, "No, nothing that you should worry about."

Bo knew he should go by Ryan's house to see what he was up to. When it was dark, Bo drove up the driveway to Ryan's house and noticed the front door open. He yelled. "Hey Ryan! You in there?" No response, so he looked around outside and observed a small trail leading into the woods. Bo, remembered that Ryan's house was only about half-a-mile from Jim's house. So he took-off down the path and found Ryan looking through a scope of a rifle pointed at Jim's house. "What are you doing?!" Bo said angrily. We re only a week away from your father s trial! Do you really want to get caught having a rifle pointed at the Amico's house? Are you <u>nuts</u>?" Ryan responded, "No, I just want to hurt him in some way!" Bo retaliated saying, "You keep this up and you ll kill any chance of getting your father out of jail!" Ryan acquiesced, "OK, OK! I'll leave him alone til the trial...but I swear I'm going to get that guy some day."

Dinner was over and Summer and Jackson did the dishes and cleaned the table and the kitchen. Jim was reading his Bible and the family gathered around him. He began reading the 103rd Psalm:

1. "Praise the Lord, Oh my soul! All that is within me, praise His Holy Name!

2. Praise the Lord, Oh my soul, and don't forget all His benefits;

3. Who forgives all our sins; Who heals all our diseases;

4. Who redeems our life from destruction; Who crowns us with loving kindness and tender mercies;

5. Who satisfies our desires with good things, so that our youth is renewed like the eagle's.

Amy looked up and said, " With all we ve gone through these past weeks, He's never stopped being our Savior and our closest friend." Jim responded, "Amen to that!" Jackson said "Why did we have to go through all this? Why did my sister go through that horrible experience? Couldn't God have stopped it all from happening? Why did our house burn to the ground and mom suffer burns? Why?"Jim looked at him and said, "God didn't stop it because He gave <u>all</u> of us free will. That means that if some of us choose to do evil things, that s part of the free will that came with His creation! God did not create us to be robots!. Instead, He wanted us to be able to choose to either love Him and accept Him by obeying the rules He s given us for our own good...or reject Him and spend Eternity in Hell without Him. His Word says in Deuteronomy 30:19,20... This day...I have set before you life and death, blessings and curses. Now choose life, so that you and your children may live and that you may love the Lord your God, listen to His voice, and hold fast to Him. For the Lord is your life, and He will give you many years in the land He swore to give to your fathers, Abraham, Isaac and Jacob.'God never said that this life would be easy. He warned us that we would face bad things, like trials and tribulations. So we can't blame Him for the evil others do. After all, the world treated Him <u>very</u> <u>badly</u>! What makes us think that the world would treat us any differently? That s why this Psalm tells us to Praise the Lord <u>always</u>! We must remember that in the Word (The Bible), Paul and Silas were put in jail. Jails in those days didn't have cots with blankets on them. No, there was nothing but dirt and rocks...and most likely, a sewer ran through the cell they were in. Their hands and feet were chained. Now <u>that s</u> a tough position to be in, one must admit! But did they cry for God to help them? No, they started to praise and worship our God! As they praised Him, their chains fell off onto the ground and the door to their cell was opened! That s what this Psalm is saying to us: no matter what condition you find yourself in, if you lift Jesus up and praise Him, your condition will change and you will see the glory of God fall!"

21

TWO DAYS BEFORE

Summer was alone in her bedroom...her eyes fixed on the two playful birds outside her window. A young woman named Summer has lived through an event that most girls her age shouldn't even conceive in their minds! Now, it s just a few days before her capturer and attacker is tried for this horrible crime! The sad thing is, she must live through that whole experience once again, an experience that would have crushed most young women, mentally and physically. Summer, however, is a different kind of woman; she is one that believes in a God that doesn't live far away, but one that never leaves her side; one that can be counted-on for strength and love like no other God can! Yes, she has a relationship with Jesus Christ. This trial has been anticipated for a long time by both the Amico family and the town of Shadow. Now that it has arrived, everyone is on edge and prepared to face the facts of that day that they ve tried to forget for so long.

The Pastor of the Church that the Amico family attends, called for a prayer-meeting for the night before the trial which was just two days away. Bo met with his fellow, crew-of-guys, to go over what would happen the day of the trial. Bo stated that working with Ryan, he developed a plan that Ryan wanted to use. There would be two explosions at the courthouse: the first would take place on the roof of the building (which was meant to shock people) and the other at the trash bin outside the room of the court- house, just below one of the windows, where the trial was taking place. That second explosion was meant to give the impression that there was a full-out-attack on the courthouse. The plan was to take Ryan's father right after the first explosion. If there was a guard protecting Ryan's father, he would be knocked-out by Ryan with a blow to the head. Ryan told Bo earlier that morning that the explosions would go off with a timing-mechanism. like a cell-phone. Bo told Ryan tha No cell-phones would be allowed in the building during the court hearings." Ryan said, "Yeah, I know...that's why someone in California will make the calls at the right time." Bo asked, "Who will that be?" Ryan said, "Don't worry, I got that covered." Each explosion would have three dynamite sticks and would make a great deal of noise with little damage. Ryan would be at his father's side during the trial and he would do the grabbing of his father. Ryan would take his father down a back stairwell and into a car that he d park out of sight two days before the trial.

Jack indicated that the plan for his crew would be to anticipate the first explosion and to get into place to stop Ryan and know that the next explosion would make everyone think that there was a full-out-attack. on the courthouse that would cause chaos in the building. The most-important-thing therefore, was to wait for Ryan to make his move first before the crew moved-in. Jack then asked, "OK, does everyone know what their job is, and are there any questions? Tomorrow we ll all go to the courthouse at the same time, along with the FBI agent, Mac Trumble, to observe a trial. We ll all go in separate cars and each of us will sit in a different area of the courtroom. We ll meet here at Bill's shop that evening to once again go over the plan. Make sure Jim will be there also." Jack wanted to know who the person was that would make the calls. Bo said, "I have no idea; it s most-likely the guy I contacted to get this job in California with Ryan." Jack interjected, "OK, that means we have no way of stopping the explosions. In that case, all personnel must be warned of the explosions and when." Bill said he d tell Mac (the FBI guy) to alert all personnel in the courthouse." Jack then insisted, "No, wait a minute...not all personnel...just the ones in the area of the explosions. It s important that Ryan is not tipped-off about our having knowledge of the break-out, or the whole thing won't work!" Bill understood and said, "Got it!"

Summer was excited to get back to school and get into the swing-of-things again. Staying close to Jackson hampered her social-time but she still managed to meet with friends. Her mind was mainly occupied with the up-coming trial, so she tried to concentrate on her studies which she was very good at. She began this school year with the study of a new language for the first time. Now that she was part of the Amico family and since she considered Jim to be her father, she decided to study Italian. Jackson on the other hand, couldn't wait to start playing football with his friends! He worked it out with Mike so he could play two hours after school with his friends in the

PB Hawks

near-by park. Mike stayed nearby, watching for
anyone who might seem suspicious. Jackson was
also a very good student, so School Work could
take place after having some fun with his friends
in the park.

Jim was still trying to find out where Ryan
might pop-up next. If he had the explosives he
needed and the timers, what else would he need?
Jim's thoughts were reeling. He began walking in
the woods across the street from his home. He
went deeper than he did before and came to the
path that Ryan used. He followed the path to a
clearing where a small cabin stood. He stayed
back and observed the house for a while when he
saw Ryan coming out of the garage and sat on
the porch-chair. He lit-up a smoke of some kind.
Jim wanted to confront him, but realized that
would destroy the whole plan; so he stayed back
and watched. Nothing much happened for awhile
until a strange man came up to Ryan's house on
foot. He was an older man and he looked familiar
to Jim, but he couldn't place him. The old man
started to talk about the trial. Ryan said to him,
"Do you know exactly what you must do at the
trial?" The man nodded and said, "I sure do!"
Ryan said, "I'm counting on you to make those
calls at the exact time we set, OK?"

"I got it...one at 9:15am and one at

9:16am...on the dot!" Ryan said,"That's right." "What about Bo?" this man asked. "I got what I wanted from him...he's expendable. I guess I'll have to kill him." "How will you do that?" the man asked. "Let me worry about that!" was Ryan's reply. "OK", the man said and went on his way.

Jim was shocked by Ryan's total-disregard for Bo's life! He had to warn Bo. He called him but no answer. He left a message to call him ASAP. Jim was frightened for Bo's life. He called Bill to see if he knew where Bo was and to tell Bill what he heard. Bill had no idea where Bo might be. He went down to the coffee shack and talked to Jack and Amy. He took Jack out on to the deck and told him what Jim heard at Ryan's place and the danger Bo was in. Jack took out his phone and called Bo and when he answered, he told Bo to drop what he was doing and meet him and Jim at the Coffee Shack immediately! Jack told him that he was in real danger so he needed to make it quick! Bo got on his bike and took-off for the Coffee Shack. As he was cruising down the road, he felt a sharp pain in his shoulder but didn't think anything about it. He got to the coffee shack, entered and went to the deck outside and sat with Jim and Jack. He started to rub his shoulder and the guys noticed blood on his shirt. "What happened?" Jack inquired. Bo replied, "Don't know, but I felt this sharp pain when I was riding down here." Jim shouted "You were shot!

Let's get you to the hospital." Jack emphatically stated, "That's why we wanted to see you! Ryan is out to kill you and it looks like he made an attempt at it while you were coming here!" They put Bo in Jim's truck and went to the hospital. When they arrived, they told the emergency doctors that Bo was shot. They knew that would bring the police and a bunch of questions. Certainly this was not what they wanted right then. So they called Mac (The FBI agent). He came immediately and was briefed about the shooting and what Jim heard at Ryan's cabin. He took complete control when the police arrived.

The bullet was shot from a high-caliber rifle and the damage was significant. Bo came very close to losing his life! The bullet lodged close to his heart and he needed to stay in bed so the doctors could determine when surgery could be performed. "That S...O...B" was Jack's outburst to Jim outside Bo's room. He came very close to dying today!"

"So there's even more to Ryan's plan! Who was this old man you saw at his place?" Mac wanted to know. "I think it's someone his family knew when they lived up here," said Jim. "The more I think about it, that old man probably owned the house that Summer was brought to when she was kidnapped! We could arrest him now but that would ruin the whole plan! How much damage would those explosives do?" Mac replied, "It s hard to tell." Jack said, "Let's keep an eye him and his house and maybe we can stop him before the second explosion!" Mac said, "Let's pretend that Bo died and put out a bulletin to the press that he died in surgery." Bill said, "I'll do it right now!" He must be kept in a safe place in the hospital. One of the doctors spoke-up and said "We have a room down in the basement that's used for quarantined. patients. He could stay there and we can still keep an eye on him."

Amy could not believe the events that had taken place by this so-called-<u>friend</u> from high school! What's next? she thought. *Will he cause another family-member to be hurt? Would he come after our children? Undoubtedly all this would hurt our business!* She asked Jim, "What next can we expect from this maniac?" Jim told her that the plan was in effect and it needed to play-itself-out. He said that they <u>all</u> just needed to stay in prayer and believe that God and His instruments (the crew-of-guys) have this under control! Jim concluded by saying, Have faith, Amy! The Lord will not let us down."

Jim gathered his family together after

dinner...they all knelt down and Jim prayed, "Father, we come to You in the name of your Great Son Jesus. You are our the most-high God, the Creator of all things! You are the great I AM and we worship You! Jesus, You left heaven and took nothing with you, not your crown or thousands of Angels bowing down in service to You. You left it all to die on a cross for the sins of each one of us. How can it be that my King would die for me? We bless Your Name, our Savior and Lord. We lift-up this situation to You and we know You are in control and that You love us beyond anything we could imagine! I ask for Your protection for my beautiful family...my wife, the daughter you gave to me, this wonderful son that I still can't believe that I have the privilege to help raise to be the man after Your own heart. I also ask Your protection for our friends, Bill and May...for those you've sent to help us in our dire need...Jack, Bo, Mike, Mac, the Police and the others. Thank You for sending the Holy Spirit as our Helper and Counselor! Thank you for all You are about to do and all You have already done for us. Amen and Amen!"

22

THE DAY BEFORE

October 14...the day was coming to a close and evening was on its way. The Amico family was going to a prayer-meeting at the church because the next day, the trial would begin. The trial-day was anticipated for a long time, but that night, the town was attending church to lift up to God all their fears and horrible memories of a day that will live with them for weeks, months and years to come. That night, they would set-aside those fears and horrible memories...that night they would share time with God, The One who will comfort and heal them with His loving hand.

Through prayer and praise, He would tell them that He is always with them and when a storm comes, He will be along-side of them...never to forget them or abandon them. He is the rock they would be able to hold on to...He will give them...peace that surpasses all understanding."They can't be separated from His love, no matter what happens! His, Comfort will overtake them and the newness of a new day will bring new mercies! They belong to Him and He will protect them until the day they go home and live with Him! These are some of the thoughts that are running through their minds...and Jim's mind.

Now some may not understand how anyone could feel these things from God. The reason is simple: they have not accepted what Jesus did on the cross for them and they have not asked Him to be part of their lives. So as hard as this may sound, they don't have the comfort and peace of knowing that their God is close and has-their-back!   This may seem too simple to think that God would be by their side and have-their-back if something were to go wrong. Christians live with what the Word says: "I will never leave you nor forsake you." And so, if God said it, He will hold to it and bring it to pass!

The Amico family had been seeking the face of

God. Ryan was dressed in black and was entering a small window which he left open when he visited the courthouse earlier that day. He climbed on a dumpster and carefully placed the backpack with the dynamite in the window and lifted himself up and into the building. He went straight to the stairs and up to the roof. He found a small trash can and placed three sticks of dynamite in it along with the cell-phone...all wired-up so that it would ignite the dynamite-bomb when the correct numbers were called. So far it was going just as he had planned it (or as Bo planned it before he was shot). Ryan then proceeded down the stairs and found the courtroom that his father would be in and checked everything out. He made sure that the stairs that he and his father would use would lead them out of the building. He put a little piece of wood in the door-frame so the door would not close all the way. He went out the same window that he came in and dropped the rest of the dynamite in the dumpster and moved the dumpster just outside one of the courtroom windows. He wondered why there was so little security and how easy it was to get into the courthouse. He didn't know that the FBI and the Shadow Police Department were watching every move he made.

Summer attended the prayer-service and she showed a good front with a smile and a warm

"Hello" to everyone. The insides of Summer were upset to say the least! Her stomach was churning with the anticipation of who she had to face once again. Those emotions were definitely taking a toll on her. As much as she tried to push the thoughts of that day away, somehow they would wind their way back into her mind. She told herself that it was just one day and that she d never have to face that evil man again.

She told herself that he'd never be able to hurt her again! She told herself that God would shield her from any further evil this man could ever do to her. Yes, she told herself all these things over and over, but the fear never went away. When she was with her family, she felt safe, especially around Jim. Her brother stood close to her and for some reason she felt he knew what she was going through. He would put his arm around her shoulder and whisper "Its going to be alright, Sis. You'll see!" She would smile and turn away...back to her thoughts of tomorrow. Then what seemed to come out of thin air...a voice spoke to her: "Summer, I am with you! Do not fear tomorrow for it will be over in a short time and you will be safe." She knew this was the voice of the Lord and suddenly she felt calm and peaceful. She truly enjoyed the rest of the prayer-meeting. When the prayer-meeting was over, the Amico family started for home to get ready for the events of the next day.

Jack went to the hospital to pick-up Bo and took him to the house they were renting. His shoulder was mending and he was feeling the effect of the drugs he was given. Jack and Mike helped him out of the car and put him to bed, which was the doctor's prescription for his recuperation. They told him they'd provide him with his meals and showed him a pitcher of ice-water on the bed-stand for something to drink. Bo asked how things were going...was everything ready for the trial. Jack told him the FBI was controlling the situation and Ryan was being watched closely. Jack said, "Tomorrow we'll all be in the courtroom, except you, and we'll be ready to execute the plan for Ryan." Bo asked, "Will the FBI allow the bombs to go off?" Mike responded, "Yes, and we're hoping no one will be hurt. Ryan's in for a big surprise!"

After placing the bombs in their designated locations, Ryan situated himself in the get-away car he hid in the parking area of the courthouse. Remember, this is Oregon, so the parking area is not a wide-open space like you would see in most cities. The courthouse parking lot was in a heavily-wooded area, so finding a place to keep a car out sight was easy. It still bothered him that the security was so insufficient; he even wondered, if they knew what he was about to do. He pulled a lever for the seat of the car to fall backwards and he lay there and eventually fell off to sleep.

Summer and Jackson were asleep in their rooms; Jim and Amy were in bed also. Jim turned off the lights and said good-night to Amy with I love you and Amy said the same, which was their custom ever since they were married. Jim's last thoughts were about a day the Amico family will have to live with for a long time. The man who brought terror to his daughter and caused her harm and disgrace will now face the punishment for his crimes.

23

TRIAL DAY

The morning brought another magnificent day with few clouds and a mist hanging in the pine trees. The view along the river revealed smoke coming from the chimneys of the homes that lined its banks. Praise was given to the Lord ...for another day He had made. The Amico s had already gotten ready for the ninety-minute drive northeast of Shadow, to the County Courthouse located in the town of Gain, Oregon. The town of Gain was much bigger than Shadow, with many more stores for shopping and a larger movie theater. It contain the County Courthouse, Federal Building that houses the FBI and other federal agencies, a large park used for bike-riding, roller-skating and of course,   fishing in the river that runs through the town. This day would be an ex-perience that would be remembered for a long while.

One thing Ryan did when he put the bombs in place was to leave a 45 caliber pistol in the men's room behind an air-vent. Ryan woke-up with a headache which he surmised was caused by the way he was sleeping in his car. He raised his seat and looked around the area where his car was lo-cated. He rubbed his eyes, looked in the back of the car and took out the suit he intended to wear, which was draped in plastic on a hanger, lying on the back seat. He opened the door of his car, felt the cool-fresh-air and started to feel alive again. With the suit in his hand, he entered the building through the window he d left open the day be-fore...went past the metal-detectors without inci-dent and on to the restroom where he washed-up with some soap he had wrapped in his suit pocket. He put on the suit and tie, took a second look around the room and opened the air-vent and took out the 45 glock he had placed there the day before. He made sure it was loaded and placed it in the back part of the waist-band of his pants...then proceeded to the courtroom. It was early and the doors to the courthouse were closed and locked. A guard stood outside the courthouse to answer questions and to keep in-line those wanting to enter. After exiting the courthouse a window (the same way he had entered) Ryan stood in the line, patiently waiting to be allowed to enter. Also in line were Jack, Mike and the FBI agent who was armed with his own 45 pistol. The waiting-line grew as more Shadow residents were arriving. Just before the doors were opened, the Amico s arrived. Amy and Jackson got in the line; Summer and Jim were immediately escorted into a witness room adjacent to the courtroom. At 9:00 am, the doors were opened and the people were allowed in to take their seats. It was a large room with windows to the right side of the judge s bench. Fans were running from ceiling-mounts which made the room comfortable. A buzz went through the room when the defendant entered on the left-side of the room facing forward. All were seated behind a wooden railing that went along the room from wall-to-wall separating the defendant, attorneys and the prosecutor from the people attending. Jack and Mike sat behind Ryan who was seated behind his father and his father s attorney. The FBI agent (Mac) sat on the right-side just across from Ryan. There were two guards with weapons on each side of the judge s bench. The defendant, Sid Knaps, entered the room with an armed guard who removed the defendant s handcuffs. A few moments later, the judge entered the court and a guard said, "All rise!" as the judge took his seat and told the crowd to be seated. Ryan wasted no time...he took out his phone to check the time which alerted Jack and Mike along with Mac. Ryan s accomplice (the old man) made the call that triggered the bomb at the roof-level. The explosion was loud and distractive as parts of the ceiling came crashing down! There was mass-confusion as people ran and screamed. Ryan took out his 45 and shot the two guards at each side of the judge's bench. It happened so fast that Jack and Mike didn't even try to stop him, but Mac (FBI agent) took out his gun and shot Ryan in the upper arm as he was grabbing his father to lead him through the designated exit door inside the courtroom...then down the stairs. The blood from Ryan's wound was pouring-out and he hesi-tated, anticipating the signal from his accomplice that would trigger the second bomb in the trash-container next to the courtroom window...or so he thought! He didn't know that the trash bin was moved during the night by the FBI and it was now located next to the exit that Ryan and his fa-ther would be going through...just as the bomb went off! The explosion was deafening and so powerful that it ripped through the dumpster-wall and a piece of metal hit Ryan in the chest, killing him instantly. His father was blown just five feet from Ryan and was captured immediately by police. The two guards that were shot by Ryan were in serious condition but were later reported to be recovering in a local hospital. No one else had been injured, which was quite a miracle in itself! The Courthouse was a mess with a partial roof-collapse and a damaged wall at the exit where the second bomb exploded. However, for an event like this to happen and not lose another human life was remarkable! The prayers that had been said for this day were heard by the Lord and His protection was all around everyone else that day. Ryan was the only one who lost his life and it was difficult not to think that perhaps he was deserving of this fate since it was all his idea for this to take place! Ryan's father didn't know all this would occur because his son never told him what was going to happen. Ryan's accomplice would later be arrested because the FBI could trace the source of the cell-phone numbers. These events left Sid Knaps in shock and the death of his son left him in tears. Still, the day was not as bad as it could have been.

Summer and Jim were in the witness room when the explosion went-off and held on to each other. When they heard the shots, Jim pulled

Summer to the floor and they waited until the shots stopped. Jim got up and pulled Summer up with him. "What just happened?" Summer cried out. "It's Ryan trying to break his father out," Jim informed her. Summer asked him, "Did you know about this?" Jim responded, "Yes I did but I had men taking care of it along with the FBI." Summer then asked, "Why didn't you tell us?" Jim explained, "Because it was better you didn't know about it until it was over! Now let s go and find your mom and Jackson!"

Many people had assembled outside the courthouse! Some of the Amico s friends found their way to the courtroom and saw Jackson and Amy who were shaken but alright! They embraced and were escorted out of the building. Jim and Summer also found Amy and Jackson, so they were all together and safe! Amy put her arms around her kids and kissed them both and turned to Jim and threw her arms around him and said, "I love you!" Jim looked at her and said, "I love you too...and I thank God for you everyday for the love you have given me!"

They were all cleared to go home; they found Bill and May and arranged to meet later for dinner to share the day s events...then got in their cars and went home. The ride was quiet but joyous and for the first time in a long time, they had nothing to worry about until someone said "Who s gonna open the Coffee Shack tomorrow?" They all said, "Not me!" and they all shared in an up-roarious, emotion-releasing laughter!

24

NEW DAY-A NEW LIFE

Seeing the beauty that is coming from the screen outside of the car window gave Summer a peace that she hadn't felt in a long time. This child of 16 years has been through an ordeal that would send most people into total downward spiral that would be hard to recover from. Summer is different she was schooled on how much she is loved by God, her family and herself. She is determined to rise above any diversity that would cause her harm. To most that is easy to say but, living it is another story.

Summer is entering into that phase that will determine her way in life. Will she be a victim or will she be a winner and overcome all of the ugliness of this tragedy. For someone as young as

Summer that road will be long and difficult. Is she wise enough to know that others will look at her differently? Some will see her as damaged, some will blank her from their minds, some will see her as broken, and some men will see her as someone not worthy of marriage. While all them have their opinions, the only opinion that matters is the Summer's opinion of herself.

As the journey home is coming to end the excitement of home overwhelms Summer. Home is safe, home is love, home is warm, home is happy, home is pleasant and right now the only place she wants to be. Summer entered the house with a glowing smile on her face that everyone asked about. Which she answered "it's just great to be home after what we just experienced." A sigh that indicated agreement, and I know what you mean came from everyone.

Jim said let's have a time of prayer, they all gathered in the living room and knelt as Jim began to pray. "Dear Father we give you praise for you are worth the highest praise. You have blessed us with your love and protection as always You have been there for us. This has been a time that we never believed we would have to go through and yet with Your arm around us we made it through. Our daughter has seen and went through something horrifying and our hearts are broken for her. Lord Your presents in her life as made her strong and able to fight off the fear that comes with this kind of happening. As strong as she is without You she will fall apart. I pray you give her the courage to fight off any attempts by the evil one to make this tragic event over-whelming. Give her the grace to overcome all that this world will throw at her. Give her insight to foresee any obstacles she will face in life. Give her courage to tell the world, if she has too, about how to overcome a tragic problem that they may have to face. Give her the ability to speak about Jesus and about His loving kindness and the fact that He said, "I will never leave you or forsake you." I pray this in Jesus Name. 'Amen.'

Summer made her way to her room, she put on her PJ's and laid down on her bed. Her mind was fixed on the pray her father just said and wondered what will the future bring? Well, she thought, I was going to Oregon U and study com-puters and after graduation I'll get the best pay-ing job I could find. I will find a good christian man and get married. It seemed so simple to her and yet she knew it would be difficult. How could I get close to a guy after what I went through, will I ever be able to trust a man or allow him to touch me. There are many things to work through and I don't think I can do this on my own. I must talk to mom and dad.

Summer awoke to the smell of bacon and pancakes and ran down to the kitchen and throw her arm around Jim and said, "I love you dad" and Jim said "I love you too sweetheart." Amy watched with joy on her face and Jim said "and I love you too Jackson" "me too dad." Well, do we open the Shack this morning? "No," Jim said "Bill and May are opening the Coffee Shack and we will go and relieve them when we are done." Summer and Jackson said "Can we come" "Why don't we all go and share the work load it will make things go easier." The breakfast was soon over and the dishes are in the dishwasher and the family was off to their Coffee Shack.

Epilogue

Evil was faced and is defeated, however, the effects of combating evil are like scares that linger and must be faced with each passing day. Summer overcame evil but the fight goes on by the effort to push thoughts away that may over-whelm your future. So the fight never ends, but as the days go on the battle seems easier with the help of the Holy Spirit. Summer, being the christian she is, never walks alone, for she is never forsaken by her God first and the people that love her.

Lets be honest, what Summer went through is not something you can forget by the use of will power. This tragedy is a battle that must be con-quered each day and by doing so she gains power to fight the next day. I realize that unbe-lievers that are read this book will not understand the relationship between a believer and their God. This difficulty is the cause of numerous incidents that in life that can only be explained by the lack of Jesus Christ in their lives. I do not try to expose Christians as perfect, we are not. A Christian understands that their Lord loves them unconditionally and they lean on Him for help and complete understanding. They turn to the one that took their place on the cross and has given them Life and that more abundantly.

So Summer will live her life not defeated, but victorious and experience the wonders life can bring by walking in the light of Christ. I am sure the world will bring her hard times, but I am just as sure that God will be by her side every step of the way and she will have more victories than defeats. She will live through high school go to college and graduate with honors, get married and have a family of her own. I can't wait to see what life will bring to this beautiful girl for Shadow.

<<<<>>>>

ABOUT THE AUTHOR.

He was born into a Brooklyn Italian family, Phil was a shy and timid Catholic young man and did not fit in with the other boys in his neighborhood. He quit school and enlisted in the US. Army, at seventeen. After his military career he continued his education. Seven years, of architectural train- ing later he started working in the profession of Architecture. It was a mystery to him how he found a life on the Oregon coast. Sitting in front of his computer he start to write which has con- tinued until this very day.

Christianity was part of his life since 1977 when he did something most Catholic's never do, he gave his life to Jesus Christ and life had mean- ing for the first time. Christian Drama Fiction is his way of bringing out the truth's of Jesus. His writings are novels that man women could under- stand and enjoy. His first book 'The visitor"was a short story of a Church longing for better things and received all they prayed for, only to lose it all because they were ashamed of the giver. His second novel "Can You Hear The Holy Spirit?" tells a story of two young men wanting to see gods power in their Church and how God answers their request. Now comes his best effort. His new book is 'Transfixed-Christian Fiction, Mystery, Romance, Family values and a Christian way of Life.

The enjoyment of writing is praying in a different way. He asked the Holy Spirit for the guidance and rejoices when the answer is revealed. The Lord will get His message out in anyway He can. He just wants be a tool in the hands of his Lord. Just like the men in his last book, he wants to see God's power demonstrated to all the church so Jesus will be Glorified.

Thank you for purchasing this book. This book will prove to be an interesting adventure for the whole family. Some other books written by PB Hawks:

The Visitor

This first book was written by Philip Beckinella and it covers what happens to a church that is in such great need that it focuses on pray. They seek God for their needs and He answers their pray. However, they lose it all because they become ashamed of the giver. Now they know the value of the giver and become the church that God always wanted them to be. Click Here and Grab a Copy

Can You Hear The Holy Spirit? - Power Rarely Seen In Today Church

Two young men, who are good friends, desired to see the wonders and miracles that early church experienced. These men decided to pray and ask God to send someone to show them the way to achieve signs and wonders that the early church had. God answered them by sending an old woodsman to show the way to the One who can delivery these signs and wonders. They soon became the focus of all the towns around the area because of the miracles that were happening all around them. Click Here and Grab a Copy

Transfixed - God | Romance | Tragedy | Family

Next to our need for God is our need for family. A California man decided to make the town of Shadow, Oregon home. Being single he never had time for women because he devoted all his time to his work, which is Architecture. He was becoming tried of big city living and wanted something like a small town to live in. Well, on vacation with a friend, he found on western side of Oregon the town of Shadow. The story of Jim and Amy's family unfolds soon after he arrives in town. The evil and the terror that is experienced by the town and Jim and Amy and Amy's daughter is overwhelming. Only their love for God and each other pulled them through this horrifying tragedy. This is the book you just finished reading.

The Master Within-The Future Is Yours To Win Or Lose

This is a book that reveals the true nature of people. We think that the answer to life is somewhere out there. The answers that most people are looking is within themselves. When stop to think about it who knows us better our self, we shouldn't ask the the outside world for answers that we can provide. This book will allow you to see yourself better than anyone else can show you

www.ingramcontent.com/pod-product-compliance
Lightning Source LLC
Chambersburg PA
CBHW070817120626

46556CB00002B/546